A HOOD Princess

An Eastside Love Story

2

A NOVEL BY

K.A. WILLIAMS

© *2019 Royalty Publishing House*

Published by Royalty Publishing House
www.royaltypublishinghouse.com

ALL RIGHTS RESERVED
Any unauthorized reprint or use of the material is prohibited. No part of this book may be reproduced or transmitted in any form or by any means, electronic or mechanical, including photocopying, recording, or by any information storage without express permission by the author or publisher. This is an original work of fiction. Names, characters, places and incidents are either products of the author's imagination or are used fictitiously and any resemblance to actual persons, living or dead, is entirely coincidental.
Contains explicit language & adult themes suitable for ages 16+ only.

Royalty Publishing House is now accepting manuscripts from aspiring or experienced urban romance authors!

WHAT MAY PLACE YOU ABOVE THE REST:

Heroes who are the ultimate book bae: strong-willed, maybe a little rough around the edges but willing to risk it all for the woman he loves.

Heroines who are the ultimate match: the girl next door type, not perfect - has her faults but is still a decent person. One who is willing to risk it all for the man she loves.

The rest is up to you! Just be creative, think out of the box, keep it sexy and intriguing!

If you'd like to join the Royal family, send us the first 15K words (60 pages) of your completed manuscript to submissions@royaltypublishinghouse.com

SYNOPSIS

Sometimes friends become foes and foes friends...

After tragedy strikes and Lyric puts her life on hold to uphold her family's name, she learns just what it means to be the royal and most hated family in the hood. Because with royalty comes a heavy and violent crown to carry.

Juggling her new life, Lyric is caught up in a dangerous game of love that can help build her empire or burn it to the ground.

With both loves of her life, Beatz and Osiris, at war, there's only one heart for the taking and Lyric's life, along with her family's, depends on her choosing the better man.

LYRIC

"You thought you could fuck with my team and get away with it?" Pop's voice was loud, filled with a rage that nobody was able to tame.

I stayed on the concrete with my heart beating like it was midnight on New Year. The bullets just wouldn't stop no matter how loud I screamed or how hard I prayed. I was so afraid to look up for fear of me receiving a bullet between my eyes.

"Oh shit!" I heard Osiris's voice and the sound of tires burning out on the concrete. When I finally looked up, I saw Osiris running towards my pop's Tahoe like somebody lit a fire to his ass. My heart stopped beating for the short ten seconds of my brain registering what was happening or had happened.

With the bit of strength I possessed, I removed myself from the concrete and ran in the direction of Osiris and Pop. When I made it over to the SUV, my hands flew to my mouth and my knees buckled.

"No, no, no!" Tears sprung out my eyes on the beat of my screaming.

"Get her back!" Osiris shouted demands at some tall, dark-skinned man. The same man that was waiting next to the truck for Pop at HQ. I guess he was a driver or guard for the crew. Whoever he was, he scooped me up like I was just some small child and carried me into the hotel lobby. Once he put me down, I ran right back outside, my eyes catching a glimpse of the scene I hadn't noticed before. There were two bodies laid out cold where Beatz's car had been.

"Nigga, get her back in there!" Osiris raised his voice louder than the first time. I respected him trying to protect me from the sight, however, I was in no kind of mood to let my pop stay out there without me.

"Don't you dare fuckin' put your hands back on me. Let me see my pop." Tears were thick in my eyes; so thick I was barely able to see anything ahead of me. The thought of Pop dying out there set my chest on fire, causing all the emotions to travel up to my throat.

Pop laid beside the truck with his hands resting beside him. Blood was dripping out his mouth, instantly staining the concrete underneath him. I dropped to my knees and placed my hands over the gunshot wound that laid exposed on his neck.

"Pop, you can't go out like this. Please, don't go out like this. Hold on, help is on the way." I said those words like I was sure somebody called for the paramedics. Like him holding on until they arrived would save his life.

"Ly-ly…" Pop tried his best to speak. Each attempt he tried to speak, the more blood he lost. He coughed a few times, struggling to breathe through the terrible gunshot wound that stared me in the eyes.

"Don't speak. Just hold on. Just hold on," I replied through tears that felt like they would never let up. "We need you Pop. I know sometimes we act like we don't, but we do. We need you here. Just stay."

"Take care of them for me, and don—" Pop spoked his last words before his breath was snatched. I removed my hands from the wound and closed his eyes. I was stuck on the concrete for what felt like forever. My body was paralyzed all over. I was aware of what kind of life Pop led, and the danger that lurked around every corner. I just never thought anybody was strong enough to snatch him away from us.

"I want every fuckin' stone in this state turned. I want that nigga dead," Osiris spoke sternly over the phone as he paced back and forward in front of the hotel. The man that was still a question to me stood next to the truck on the phone, too.

Nobody had to tell me a damn thing; I knew a war started. The entire state was about to feel the wrath of the Eastside Warriors' honcho being dropped dead. I was going to be sure of it.

With all the commotion going on around me, my mind fell on Beatz. A bitter rage I had never known filled my lungs. It grabbed me so tight around my soul, I thought I would die. The boy that was my friend since we were in kindergarten betrayed me in the worse way possible. He was the reason I was going to be burying my pop in the coming week. The reason why I had to step up, take over the empire and make sure my pop's legacy lived on.

"I don't want him dead. I want to see him personally," I told Osiris. He looked over at me as if he was viewing a monster. Standing there, that's exactly what I felt like. I was going to lash out at everybody that stepped at me the wrong way. I had to watch out for my family now, step up in the shoes and do all the things Pop did over the years. The Eastside Warriors were mine for the taking.

* * *

"WHERE'S LEX?" I stood in the waiting room waiting for Momma and Boni to be released. They said they were fine and no damage was done to their lungs from smoke inhalation. They would be released without any restrictions. Once they were in my presence, I had to tell them that Pop was gone. He was dead and never coming back.

"She went down the hallway. Don't worry Axe is right on her heels for her protection," Osiris said. Since the ambulance picked up Pop from the hotel, Osiris had been quiet, minus the few phone calls he made. He put a price on Beatz's head, a price I made him drop.

"Last I checked, Axe ain't do a good job protecting Pop," I said out of the bitter aftermath of losing my pop. I wanted to lash out. "So, why the fuck is the nigga still breathing? I want him dead."

"Lyric, none of us did a good job of protecting Don. Because if we did, he would still be here. Now if dropping the whole gang makes your loss easier then I'm all for it." Osiris leaned against the wall like he'd given up on life. It wasn't the time for anybody to fold. We were in need of the entire crew turning rough on Pop's behalf. Get the revenge he deserved.

"You vouching for that nigga?" I stepped to Osiris's face. Him taking up for somebody wasn't in any favor of mine.

"I ain't vouching for no nigga. I'm just speaking facts. It's all our fault. We should've been more ahead of the game. Should've forced Don to go in hiding while we take care of the streets," Osiris replied while looking dead at me.

"Nigga you know what, I don't real—" I stopped in mid-sentence. Well, in the middle of me about to rip Osiris apart with words, Momma and Boni walked into the waiting room looking like they had the toughest day of their lives. And knowing they almost died in a shitty ass house fire, I knew that was an understatement.

"Where's Don? I thought he was coming to pick us up?" Momma looked from me to Osiris then back to me waiting on some answers.

"I need you to have a seat." Tears welled in my eyes as I was on the verge of breaking the worse news a person could break. My momma lived and breathed Pop. Although he did some shitty things to her, she never stopped loving him. She tolerated all his wrongdoing because love has a way of keeping you in most situations even when your mind is telling you to run for the hills.

"No, don't do it. Don't. Don't. Don't." Momma placed her hands on top of her head. She strolled around the room on the verge of pulling her sisterlocs out. Boni was six years under me, and she was sheltered more than any of us at that age. I didn't expect her to know what I was about to say off bat, or to even understand me completely. Whenever Pop wasn't losing his mind over the gang or just being malicious, Boni was his heart. He took her places that he never took us. They were practically conjoined at the hips.

"He was gunned down at the hotel earlier this morning." I allowed the words to rip from my soul. In the middle of me telling them what happened, Lex walked back into the room with Axe. "He was killed."

"No." Momma placed her hands over her mouth. She dropped to her knees without a scream escaping her mouth. She just rocked back and forward on the floor. Lex grabbed Boni into her arms and within a few seconds, we were all in tears.

I was the one in charge; I had to bring us all peace. However, I was so damn clueless about gang violence that I was going to need an advisor, and there was no one better than Osiris. It's how things were going to be anyway once Pop stepped down. But instead of smooth sailing into my new position, I had to put on rollerblades and skate my way into it.

"Who did this? Who had the nerves to murder Don?" Momma screamed through the tears. Her words hit me deeper than anything. It split my heart all over again because I knew the truth. I knew the one person that I loved betrayed me. He took my pop's life in front of me.

"That's what we're trying to find out," I said.

Osiris looked at me in suspicion of why I stood there holding back information. I had my reasons though. I didn't want anybody putting a price on Beatz's head or getting to him before my men did. It was my duty to make hell open on him, and to make him feel the wrath of taking someone who meant so much to me.

Standing there dwelling on everything that lied ahead of me, my mind thought up the most malice revenge to make Beatz suffer at my hand the same way he'd made Pop. To take someone he loved to ease my own pain. To have the one person who looked out for him banished from the earth while he watched.

Murdering someone who lived on the Eastside was against code; against the old code. But I wasn't my pop and in his last breath of life, he told me to take care of my family. Part of taking care of them was to somehow make them sleep better at night knowing I was doing something about it.

"I don't understand. I don't understand." Momma punched the floor until her hands were leaking blood. Osiris had to go over to restrain her before she was suffering from injuries that would keep her up at night.

"It's gon' be aight. We gon' get who's responsible for this." Osiris wrapped his arms around Momma as he spoke with assurance in his tone. In the beginning, he was really no one to me, but in that waiting room, I loved him more than ever. He stole my heart without having to say a word. It was about how much he cared for my family that trapped me in his web. Because most men were busy worrying about a woman without caring for her family. Osiris was every bit of different. He was a man. A man that found favor in my eyes and with him beside me, we were going to make the streets bloody.

BEATZ

⚜

"What the fuck was that?" I tossed the desk chair against the wall. Lyric invited me to come to see her and that's what I did. I got my happy ass dressed and headed up there to see if she was alright. Then not a minute after I saw her pretty ass walking out of the hotel, Don pulled up and started some shit. It was like the whole damn thing was a setup to get me up there. For the nigga to off me. I lost two of my men in the crossfire and in the middle of all that shit, I had to fend for my damn self if I wanted to walk out alive. Don was shooting to kill, so it was a dog eat dog world out there. Kill or be killed type of shit. So, I just grabbed a damn gun and went to shooting. And to my surprise, I shot Don. Messed him up bad. But a part of me wanted to instantly run to his aide for Lyric's sake. Our friendship, our relationship, all of it was ruined on my account. We were no longer friends; we were enemies living in the same town.

"How the fuck did he find out? I thought you said the cameras were wiped clean, dawg? You set me up nigga? Huh? You set me up?" I yelled at T-Max. There was nobody else I could take the anger out on. It was just him standing in that damn office happy as hell Don was dead. He kept telling me that I won, and I didn't have anything to worry about. He was wrong, though. I had a whole lot of shit to worry about. They marked me as public enemy number one to the Eastside Warriors and I knew they weren't going to stop until they had my head and make me pay for taking Don from them and his family. I knew Lyric wasn't going to let the shit rest for a second; not long as the right hand of Don was still roaming the streets and in close with her. None of them was going to allow me to rest.

"You need to calm the fuck down. This tantrum isn't helping a damn thing. You need to be thinking 'bout your next move." T-Max kept his composure through his entire reply. It made me want to knock his teeth down his throat. Like how the hell was he able to remain calm when we were the center of all the gangs' attention for murdering Don? The 211 Vipers was probably the most talked about gang in the state, and news in the Boot spreads like a wildfire.

"Calm down? Naw, I'm not gon' calm the fuck down. I'm in hot water right now. I lost the girl that I loved since forever, I shot her dad while she was right there, and she won't ever forgive me." My head felt like it was going to explode from the headache that raged at my temples.

"Fuck the lil' bitch. You should be patting yourself on the back. You did something that all these niggas on the street wish they were able to do. And if I checked, you ain't murder anybody, you killed the nigga out of self-defense. It was going to be either you or him. That's how it is out here," T-Max said.

"Fuck!" I walked out of the office with the burning sensation of plasma boiling through my veins. Just couldn't shake Lyric form my mind. Her hating me left a numbness in my heart.

"There goes the man," Jay said as he met me at the bottom of the stairs. Since I made it back to HQ, everybody had been walking up to me and congratulating me on killing Don. It was like I was God in their eyes. Everybody's phones were ringing off the hook wanting to know the details and if it was true or not. I was in no damn mood to tell anybody what happened. I made sure my men kept their mouths closed until further notice.

"Mannn, cut it out." I brushed Jay's words off. Back at the hotel, Jay was with me. He was with me when Don came out of nowhere and started firing at us. He knew the whole story. I just had to make sure he didn't say shit to the wrong people. "It's not that big of a deal and don't be running with that shit either. Keep your mouth closed."

"Alright, but you the man. I ain't think you were going to hit 'em, but you proved me mad wrong. All respect, boss. All muthafuckin' respect." Jay said what he had to say then he went on by his business.

Being at HQ wasn't giving me any mind of thinking room. T-Max was all in my face about hashing out another plan. Gang members were all in my face talking about Don and the Eastside Warriors. It's like every corner I turned there was another nigga in my face. Like niggas flocked to me like Jesus walking in the flesh. They were praising me.

"Aye boss, you have a phone call." T-Max caught up with me before I was able to make a run for it and make my way off the premises.

"A phone call for me?" I questioned. I swear I sounded like some kid when I asked that question. A kid who wasn't important at all and a sudden phone call popped up for him.

"Yeah it's Wayne," T-Max said.

I grabbed the phone and said, "What's up?"

"So, you're now known as the lil' honcho who banished Don. I can't say I saw that shit coming…" There was a sudden pause before Wayne continued with the conversation. "Come over to my crib this weekend for a celebration for your accomplishment. All expenses are on me."

"Yeah, I don't know 'bout that. Me and my crew were planning our own little victory party." I caught T-Max's frown as I spoke over the phone. That lie came out of my mouth quicker than any truth ever had.

"Well, we can just come over there," Wayne said.

"You said all expenses on you though, right? So, we'll just come to your spot," I replied, noticing how hard I held the phone in my hand when a slight crack ran down the screen.

"I knew that would catch your attention, but T-Max already knows the address. It's all the way up this weekend my boy." Wayne's voice blasted from the speakerphone.

"Already." I ended the call and handed the phone back to T-Max. "I'll be back later. I need to get out of here."

"You can't go anywhere alone after what you did. Are you fuckin' insane?" T-Max tucked the phone away without paying attention to the nip I caused from holding it too tight. "You probably have a price on your head right now and being caught alone is what they praying on."

"I said I need some space." I moved past T-Max, failing to listen to his advice.

"You better get used to this shit," T-Max yelled out.

***

My momma sat on the sofa in front of the TV with tears running down her cheeks. I decided against asking her what the hell was wrong because she normally cried watching Soap Operas. I remember almost having a heart attack one day when I walked into her room and saw her hard-down crying, only to find out it was because of some favorite character of hers died on an episode.

"You heard Don was murdered outside of the Horseshoe? There's an open investigation going on right now for the shooter responsible. They say somebody just jumped out the car and gunned him down." Momma sniffled through each word like she was losing her damn mind.

"That's not what the fuck happened. Why people making all these fuckin' rumors?" My voice was louder than the TV she had up to the max volume. After realizing what I said, I had to clear that shit up before she found out I knew something. Even worse, found out I was the one who pulled the trigger. "I mean, don't nobody know what really happened."

"The fact is, he's dead because of gang violence and malice. Are you woke now? A man as feared as Don is dead no matter how much money he put into the hood or how good he was to people after all the shit he did. A person's past always comes back." Momma wiped her eyes with the Kleenex quick as her hands allowed. "Can't you see? You're just messing up your life."

"I'm not that nigga, and I ain't come here to even talk 'bout my life. I just came to pack up my shit." Going over there was to get my mind off what happened back at the hotel. But she brought all that shit back time I walked through the door. Then it was all on the news. Local officials were investigating his death. I hadn't thought about the cameras that be at the front of the hotel until I heard there was an investigation. It was too late to double back up there because if there was any kind of footage, I knew the cops already had it in their possession. If they were really investigating the case, my ass was going to the slammer.

"Rashard, don't stand in my house and disrespect me when I'm trying to help you. I'm trying to help you." Momma stood up from the couch. I knew she wasn't in favor of my word usage towards her, but she was stepping in my space a bit too much. She birthed me and all that shit, however, she had no right trying to cripple me. Besides, her words couldn't help me now. I had the blood of the Eastside Warriors' honcho on my hands.

"My name is Beatz; I don't answer to anything else. And this conversation is over. I have to pack." I left her standing in the living room lost for words. I couldn't stay in her house if I wanted to. Hell was burning over on me now.

Being in my room after a few days made me feel homesick. I wanted to be that square nigga that nobody really knew about again. Make dope ass beats and drop songs. I wanted to be that nigga before T-Max suckered me into joining the 211 Vipers as their honcho. Take me back to the day I saw Lyric drooling over Osiris at the Shoe Toss. Go over there to her and handle the situation a whole lot different.

"Fuck bruh." I sat on the bed. My entire body trembled from a ruthless anxiety attack that grabbed me and refused to release me from its grip. "What have I done?"

T-Max told me during one of our teach and learn sessions, that the first person you kill would be on your conscience for a while until the person behind the trigger learned how to turn off emotions. That I could wake during the night due to the victim's face lurking in my dreams. He didn't tell one lie either because my brain kept repeating what happened. I kept seeing myself behind the trigger and the way Don dropped to the concrete after I got a clean shot.

The thought of Don ridding my conscience for who knows how long, made my stomach tie in a chain of knots. Worry was going to be the death of me, and possibly my downfall in the game.

OSIRIS

I didn't want to leave Lyric and her family's side after what happened to Don, and though Lyric never said it out loud, I knew she partially blamed herself for Don's death. Because if she never told Beatz where she was at, he and Don would've never been face-to-face that day. It appeared fate brought them together only to take him from us.

I tried being there every step of the way to make their grief a bit easier. After receiving a call from my Mom Duke and being on edge all day, Lyric told me to go be there for her. She told me they were going to be fine back at HQ. She claimed it would give her more time to get to know the team and to hash out a plan to get her, our revenge, on Beatz.

When I was rolling down the hood with my windows down, I got a glimpse of the fuck nigga. I couldn't make a move on him though, not in the public's eye. It was part of the Eastside code. We never brought trouble to our own hood like that. Never. Not unless we really had to. But I did blow the horn at the nigga and threw up the Eastside gang sign. By doing that, I knew it put pressure on him.

When I pulled into Mom Duke's driveway, there were two other cars parked up front. I hopped out the car in a flash. I hadn't seen her since the day she got her test results. I wasn't there to hold her hand through whatever news she received. But to see she had company made me a bit uneasy. We talked about things in private. That's what we did since I was a small boy.

"I was wondering when you were going to show up lil' boy," Tara said before I got in the house good. The reality of Mom Duke's illness slapped me in the face when I laid eyes on my sister.

"Oh damn. I wasn't expecting to see you here." I embraced Tara. I hadn't seen her since four Thanksgivings ago. She moved upstate New York in hopes of getting her writing career off the ground. My sister always had a way with words, she just wasn't getting the type of recognition she deserved, due to being in a small town.

"Well I'm here," Tara said once I released her from my embrace. She moved away from home when she turned eighteen, and that NYC environment was kind of causing her southern accent to fade a bit.

"Is Oisin here too?" I asked. My brother was the better version of me. He was a family man and a graduate with two degrees in Business Management. He lived out in Atlanta like a lot of successful black men living the dream of a hardworking man. I was no kind of resemblance of my siblings. They were making money legitimately, while I was still doing the same shit I'd been doing since ten years ago. We were all two and three years apart, with our older brother, Timber being the oldest and placing me as the youngest. With good examples in front of me, I should've let Timber's death go and gotten my shit together like my brother and sister. But my older brother had such an influence on me that no one else was able to break. I looked up to him as a father figure over the years. He looked out for all of us and all I wanted to do was make him proud by getting his revenge. It's crazy what runs through a young nigga's mind.

"Yeah, he's here. He just went over to Jab's house to see him," Tara said.

"Oh ok. Cool," I replied. If I was being completely honest with anyone, it was cool seeing my sister there and doing well. But my mind wasn't on anyone else except my Mom Duke. I needed to see her more than anybody in the world, and ask her forgiveness for having to leave her like that. "Where's Mom Duke?"

"She back there lying in bed. She wasn't feeling too good this morning and went to lay down. She has been in bed ever since. The Hospice supposed to be coming tomorrow." Tara said all those words without a lick of emotions in her eyes. I figured maybe she did all the crying on her way down and couldn't feel anything else.

"Hospice?" I questioned.

"Yeah. You know the people that come out when someone is dy—" I cut Tara off before she went too hard down explaining anything to me.

"I know what it is. I just don't know why they coming out here. She's going to be straight. You should know that." I walked away from Tara trying to hold all my emotions inside. Breaking down in front of her was the last thing I needed. I couldn't really break down in front of no one.

Mom Duke was laying in her bed watching TV when I walked into her room. She looked worse since the other day. It looked like somebody drained all the blood from her face. It had only been three days since; just three days and she already took a turn for the worse.

"Mom Duke." I kneeled next to her bed. I placed her hands in mine. It didn't feel right; that moment was foreign to me. I never went through anything like that. It pained me to know that she'd been sick all those years and I never noticed. I never noticed a vicious sickness had been killing her for so long.

"My baby," Mom Duke whispered. I would never be arrogant to say it to my siblings' faces, but I was hands down my Mom Duke's favorite. I couldn't help but be after sticking by her side for so long. After all the shit I took her through, we came back out on top and our bond was stronger than ever.

"Yeah. I'm here Ma." I knew she was in pain; she had to be. I knew guns took a nigga's life quick. However, cancer ate at the body until it was strong enough to take over the host. Nothing about death scared me. I was only afraid for my Mom Duke. I was angry, too. She was a good woman; her heart was pure. "You gon' be straight."

There was a sudden silence in the room before Mom Duke fully opened her eyes to see me. It was like she gained a quick burst of energy. She sat upright in the bed. I admired how strong she was being in my presence, in all our presence. She wasn't laying around crying her eyes out or questioning God. She was just dealing with the hand she was dealt the best she knew how.

"It's stage four breast cancer, and although my doctor is willing to treat me, I don't want to take the treatment. I don't want to do any radiation or chemotherapy. I just want to spend my last days with my family, not trying to fight not to see my last days." Mom Duke reached for the small, white bucket that sat on the nightstand and she vomited like she was on her last leg. I felt sick to my stomach just watching her vomit five times in under three minutes.

She set the bucket back on the nightstand and tucked herself under the covers as her body trembled as if the air was blasting inside of the house. I wanted her to live, and if the doctors were offering to treat her then she should've been running towards the treatments.

"I think you should let the doctors help you. It might work." I stood from my knees. I had to get some fucking air after she laid all that on me. She laid it on me that she was basically dying and wasn't going to try to get any help.

"Siris, cancer has traveled beyond my breast at this stage. My entire body is suffering now. I don't have time to be going back and forth to appointments, and losing all my hair from the treatments. If I'm gon' die, then I want to die at my own comfort with hair on my head. Just respect my decision." Mom Duke closed her eyes. She was on her way back to sleep.

*　*　*

"So, you still in that gang mess huh?" Oisin didn't give me time enough to even greet him. He just came at me the wrong way. The nigga hadn't even been home to see Mom Duke in forever and was already trying to judge everybody he thought was underneath him. I respected my brother; it was my brother who didn't respect me.

"Hello to you too," I greeted. Jab was just blazing. He never minded anybody judging him and neither did I. He was being himself and that's what I was doing.

"I heard Don is dead. Wasn't he like your boss or something? You can get out the streets now I suppose," Oisin said.

"Don was more than a boss of mine. He was a respected man throughout the state. He contributed to this neighborhood; to the entire community. He did right by his people." I defended Don's legacy. Oisin had some damn nerves speaking on something that he was completely clueless about. I gave both he and Tara their props because they beat the muthafuckin' odds. They were no longer a product of the hood. "And who the fuck asked you to be all up in my business? We both grown men out here."

"I just figured that's what you would want since, you know, you're a grown ass man. You're still living off Mom. You're almost thirty, Osiris. It's now time to let the streets go. God just offered you your ticket out," Oisin said.

I saw Jab out the corner of my eye with his eyes bucked. Anybody that had been kicking it with me for the last seven years or so knew how my anger boiled. If I never found a way to tame my temper, Oisin would've been on his back in the dirt like a real country nigga getting his ass mopped across the ground.

"I'm not living off nobody. You better get your facts straight bitch nigga, because she ain't have to work in five years. I been holding everything down, paying her back for all she did for me as a young nigga on the block. Trust me, I've given more than you ever have. And bitch I'm done talking to you." I reached for the cigarette lighter from Jab and fired up a blunt that had been calling my name all damn day. Our Mom Duke was technically on her deathbed and Oisin was busy being a damn fuck nigga. Getting on my case instead of sticking together during a time like that. It's what Mom Duke wanted. She wanted us to get along, to lean on each other.

"You want to take a hit uptight nigga?" I blew loud smoke in Oisin's face.

"No, I can't," Oisin replied with his hands in the air as if I was holding a gun at his face.

"What they do to niggas in Corporate America? Are all of you niggas uptight and shit, like y'all wearing a thong?" I took another whiff of the blunt. It was nothing like smoking on a fat blunt when I was dealing with a lot of shit.

"Bruh." Jab burst out in laughter at my smart-ass remarks towards Oisin. I was wondering when his ass was going to say a single word after I went off on Oisin. "A thong though?"

"Yeah. That's what the nigga acting like he wearing. All uptight and shit, probably wearing a pink one." I turned the blunt back to Oisin and that time he accepted. We all had a long ass journey ahead of us, especially me. I had to deal with my Mom Duke dying and trying to help Lyric get through losing Don at the hand of a trusted friend.

LEX

I snuck out HQ when everybody was sleeping, and the guards were busy talking to each other about what happened. If I was a threat, I could've offed everybody inside of there. I was on a mission to make my way back to the Eastside of Mansfield. Back to the block that was my home. Pop was dead; Beatz beat me to the punch. Not that I really was going to go through with it anyway. I thought long and hard about it for a good second, and realized I didn't want him dead after all.

It was like around three in the morning when I made it down to the Eastside. I took Pop's black Tahoe, the one he died beside. If he didn't do much, he taught me how to drive. Let me drive him around the town a few times. It hit me when he was gone that we didn't have the closest relationship. He lived under the same roof as me, but I still felt like he was a stranger. Parts of his life was one big ass secret. Just a blur.

"Can you come outside?" I parked two houses down from Moomoo. She was second in line to Michael as my friend. I never opened up to her like I did with Michael, but that morning I just needed somebody to talk to. And she, above everybody, was a good listener.

"Outside?" Moomoo questioned, a slight pause in her words. "It's three in the morning."

"I know, I just need somebody to talk to." I turned the engine off and leaned the seat back. My mind was in a million places. I'd cried all the tears that I could. Death hit the block hard; it was hitting back to back. Losing Michael took a toll on me, then to hear that my pop was gunned down outside of the hotel and didn't make it, stomped me into the dirt. "Can I talk to you?"

"Okay. Where you at?" Moomoo finally gave in to my need to vent.

"I'm just two houses down. I'm in a black Tahoe," I replied.

"Give me five minutes." Moomoo ended the call.

I sat in the truck for a good three minutes before I went to search for some weed. I was in desperate need to escape. I knew my pop used to blaze occasionally. He used to smoke whenever we drove around the town. We were hot boxing, although he wasn't aware of it. The smoke had me gone a handful of times. I played it off though, played it off so good, he fired it up every time we drove around.

"Damnit." I gave up the search.

TAP. TAP. TAP.

I looked around at the front passenger's window only to see Moomoo standing beside the SUV wrapped in a blanket like it was twenty degrees outside. We were still at the beginning of summer, well almost at the first day. When she used to come over to Michael's house whenever we invited her to hang out, she complained about the air. Moomoo was always cold. I told her to see the doctor or something because the shit wasn't normal at all.

"Don't be making all that noise," I said.

"Damn, alright." Moomoo closed the door without making too much noise. Waking somebody up in the wee hours wasn't my kind of style, especially if it wasn't Michael. It wasn't Michael, and would never be him again listening to me late in the night. "I'm sorry 'bout what happened to Michael and to Mr. Don. I've been trying to reach you without any luck."

"Are you comfortable with making a stop to the Southside with me? I can't talk 'bout this without something to take the edge off," I said. The Southside wasn't all restricted from the Eastside; it was just whenever somebody from the Eastside showed up over there, they were prepared to do whatever. Shoot them and ask questions later. That's how it was on every block when unfamiliar faces approached their territory.

"Yo, Michael and Mr. Don was just dropped, you think it's safe to go over there?" Moomoo acted tough around her other friends. With me, she was different; she never tried to put on a tough act or to make me think she was a hood chick at heart. "I just don't think it's a goo…" Moomoo trailed off when her eyes fell to the Glock 19 9mm that I retrieved from the console. It wasn't the pretty looking pistol Michael gave me as a gift for my protection, but it was going to get the job done.

"I got us. I just need a zip." I turned the engine on. Moomoo was lost for words to protest her reasoning of why it wasn't safe for us to be out that time of the morning trying to buy some weed. I pulled away from the curving and pressed the pedal to the metal like the cops were chasing me. Pop had told me many times, during our driving sessions, how to dodge niggas who were following me. He told me how not to panic, and if niggas started blasting bullets at the car to just keep my head focused on the mission.

"So, what happens now? Like with the Eastside Warriors and all the things Mr. Don had going on for the block?" Moomoo asked. I wasn't sure how to even answer her question. All I knew was that Lyric stepped up as the honcho and they were still trying to figure everything else out. She was trying to be strong for all of us, when I knew better than anybody that she was falling apart inside. Her best friend turned lover was the reason we were in our situation. He turned his back on Lyric and the block. He was a traitor to the entire block.

"Lyric is leading the Eastside Warriors now; they're hashing a plan as we speak. Things are going to work out just fine." I was barely sure of my own words. Lyric still had a lot to learn about the streets. She was older than me, but I was sure I knew more about street life than her. Like, she tried living on the edge, but she always ended up being a square though, whether she realized it or not.

"Lyric is leading them? Like, they falling in line for her?" Moomoo sounded surprised. I don't know why when everybody in the hood, minus the enemies, showed mad respect to my pop and our family for years. They were basically bowing to our feet when they saw us on the streets or anywhere in public. I couldn't go to the store without being recognized by somebody. Or them asking about Pop. His name was big among the town.

"Yeah. They fell in line for her. They're loyal to the team; to my pop's legacy." It hadn't been a good ten minutes and I was already pulling up to the Southside territory. They barely had streetlights over there, which made it hard as fuck for my blind ass to see, although I wasn't technically diagnosed with any kind of eye problems.

"Well that's good. Long as y'all still have the territory, we'll all be good. Can't imagine somebody else stepping up." Moomoo scrolled through the phone like she was going to speed dial the cops soon as she saw trouble. Pop always told us to never run to the cops. Whatever problems we had with a person; we dealt with it on our own terms. Whether somebody was out to harm us or not, we weren't supposed to run. We had our own law system. The Eastside Warriors were the officials in the hood and they got whoever, whenever.

* * *

"You know we don't sell to any Eastside niggas or bitches, so turn your ass around and head back to where you came from." Allen barked at me like a stray dog. Michael and Allen were cool on the low. That's where Michael always purchased his weed. I even met Allen on a few occasions, and he never led on to have a problem with me. All of it was new to me standing on his porch like I was some damn crackhead.

"Really? Michael used to come here all the time to buy weed and everything under the sun. Don 't give me that bullshit. I just need something to take the edge off. I'm dealing with some shit right now. I would've purchased on the Eastside, but people talk too much around there." I looked back at the SUV. Moomoo had the lights on inside and I saw her staring hard as hell at me.

"You ain't no damn Michael though," Allen said.

"Yeah. I'm not," I replied.

He peeped his head further out the door, swung the door open and let me inside. Going inside of a place alone was against the laws of the Eastside Warriors. We never stepped foot in enemies' territory without a guard by our side. I had lost so much; I couldn't make myself uphold the law. The same law that would've saved Michael's life had I followed them.

"Didn't your old man just got dropped? You know niggas still 'round lurking right? Daddy ain't here to save you now. A nigga can catch you slipping and fuck you out until they break your soul." Allen opened a white plastic box that sat on the scuffed wooden table that barely stood. "Beat you and fuck you all over again until you surrender."

"I'm not scared of a damn thing, bruh. The first sign of a nigga trying some fuck shit, I pull out the Glock and shoot to kill." I pulled out the Glock 19 to show Allen I was serious. I wasn't just some young, dumb bitch who walked the streets thinking I was untouchable. I don't know why he figured such when my pop was the realest OG that ever fuckin' walked. Although me and Pop stopped seeing eye-to-eye in his last days of life, I would forever uphold his name because I was part of him, and his name lived through his children.

"Ohh shit. Aight, put that away." Allen's eyes were wide. I learned quick that I had to be a hard nigga on the street and not some girly bitch. I was willing to wrestle in the mud with the most violent nigga at any moment to prove I wasn't to be fucked with.

"I'm just letting you know not to underestimate me." I kept the gun out just in case Allen was one of the niggas who thought he could try me.

"You want heroin, coke or just plain ole weed?" Allen looked over at me, his eyes still too focused on the Glock.

"I don't do all that other shit. Just give me a zip of weed." I already had the money ready. I never accompanied Michael when he purchased weed on the Southside, but he never kept me in the dark on the prices.

"Five dollars?" Allen viewed the money like it was a disease.

"Five for a zip. That's all I'm paying for." I stood behind my decision. Michael told me to always keep my eyes and ears open when buying weed from niggas because some tried getting over on a newbie.

"More like ten lil' shawty." Allen was in the middle of putting his product up and handing me the five.

"Bitch, I said five. Don't make me blow your brains out in your house and make it look like a suicide. Don't test me nigga. Matter fact, give me two more zips and two packs of Cigarillos. I know you have some on hand." I handed him the extra money while he quickly retrieved the items I requested. After spending too much time in there, I was finally heading back to the SUV with the items that were going to take my mind off a lot of shit. Moomoo stood near the passenger's door with her phone in her hands like she was contemplating whether to the cops or not.

"I thought a bitch had to come save you." Moomoo hopped in the truck on beat. I pulled out the driveway on a mission to get our asses back to the Eastside in one piece. Moomoo's grandma was strict. If she found out Moomoo was out that hour of the morning without her permission, she would've had a fit. Moomoo told me a while back that her grandma buried her momma on her eighteenth birthday after hanging with the wrong crowd back when Moomoo was only like two. So, she made it her life mission to raise her granddaughter the right way, even though she still lived in the same hood.

"Save me? How the fuck was you going to do that?" I laughed at the thought of Moomoo running up in there trying to be a tough guy. She would've gotten her shit bashed in without getting a lick in.

"I don't know. I was going to try though." Moomoo focused on rolling the blunts. I don't care what nobody said, she was the best at rolling up. Had that bitch looking like it was bought from the store or some shit. Imported across the border.

"You gon' be straight though, Lex? You have me a bit worried. Like, you never really opened up with me like this, you know, spend this kind of time. I just want to be sure you're not going off the deep end." Moomoo licked the blunt closed.

"Bitch, I been on the deep end." I started on the longest conversation of my life without a lick of fear of her running to tell my truth to the world. Losing Michael and Pop was enough to turn anybody rough, to make a bitch so reckless she couldn't see any oncoming traffic.

LYRIC

Osiris was back and forward between the HQ and home. His momma was bad off he told me a few days ago. I told him to be there for her and not to worry about us. Unlike me with Pop, he had the chance to really sit down with his momma during her last days. He knew she was going to eventually leave. While my pop was snatched out of the blue, I wasn't prepared to say goodbye like that. He lived on the edge his entire life. I was sure he knew the day would come one day. It just caught everybody slipping.

However, since hearing the honcho of the Serge Gs wanted to meet with me, Osiris made it his business to make it to tag along. He told me straight up that I would never go any place like that without him. He mentioned the bad blood that existed between the Serge Gs and the Eastside Warriors, but he couldn't go into much detail because whatever it was happened before he was the right hand of the Eastside Warriors. He just knew they weren't to be trusted. It was what got the 211 Vipers' honcho banished.

"Let that nigga do all his talking before you elaborate on anything. Since Don is dead, I'm sure he thinks our crew is vulnerable, but we far from that. Far from it," Osiris spoke in an aggressive tone. "Understood?"

"I hear you Siris," I said.

"Naw, but are you listening though? If we're going to hold our top spots, we have to work as a team. This is hard on all of us. I will never stop trying to get that through your head. But together we will still thrive out here." Osiris stood next to the door while I sat at the desk. All those years, I never knew how organized the drug business was or how many laws gangs followed. It was more than people slanging dope on the streets or gunning each other down. It was an actual fuckin' business that brought all kinds of money home, along with a lot of enemies attached to it. The drug industry was big enough for everybody to eat, but niggas wanted to be greedy and keep the bread to themselves. It was cutthroat.

"I'm listening Siris. I'm not dumb, okay? I've been listening to your every fuckin' word. You been bossing me around so much. You should just sit your ass behind this desk and call all the fuckin' shots since I can't give my opinion on anything." I stood from the chair to move around for a bit. I'd been at the desk all damn day going over shipment paperwork and trying to learn more about the business; Osiris putting me on game and all that shit. My soul longed to grieve for my pop, but there was so much work in front of me that made me unable. All the work hindered me from breaking down. It gave me a little strength. He told me to protect my family and those words stuck with me. I had to be strong.

"Naw, you gon' continue to sit your ass on that throne. This is your crew; I'm just feeding you valuable information." Osiris finally calmed his nerves. He talked a bit softer towards me. His words didn't hang in the air any longer. He was talking to me like we were at the same level and not like I was some dumb child. "This is all yours, Lyric. Don wanted this for you."

"What happens to all of this if somebody get you too?" Losing Pop put all kind of thoughts in my head. The crew would've gone right downhill if something happened to Osiris. Wasn't anybody going to put me on game like him and although he made my ass itch from all the talking he did, I knew he was looking out for my best interest at heart.

"Nothing is going to happen to me. I'm here. They can't get me, Lyric. They won't catch any of us slipping again. When we shoot, we will shoot to kill; no mercy. Nothing." Osiris walked over to me. He grabbed me into his arms. He felt so strong. A man like that only came around once in life. His loyalty, the love that shined in his eyes for me. Only me. His heart bigger than all the obstacles in front of us. He walked around the streets with his chest poked out, but behind closed doors, he was more than that. He had so much passion within him. So much passion it set my soul on fire. Being with him made me forget for a moment that the world was burning underneath us.

"How are you so sure?" He was close to me when I said those words and it made my pussy jump. Just days ago I felt wrong wanting to be with him in that way while I was grieving. I realized though, I had nothing to be ashamed of. It was normal to vent and find comfort in another person.

"I'm just sure." Osiris wrapped his right hand gently around my throat. His dominance sent me over the top before we even started. I longed to feel him inside of me. To give him a part of me I never gave to another man. He was receiving the real vulnerable side of me. It wasn't in the moment sex; it was all infused with passion, guided by loyal sex. It was pure in its own way.

"You make me so weak," I said through a low moan.

"Is that so wrong?" Osiris focused on removing my underwear from underneath the mini dress with his left hand while his right hand still wrapped around my throat. When he replied to me, a surge went through my body; a surge that only he was able to tame.

"No," I whispered.

"Good," Osiris said.

Once my underwear was down to my ankles, Osiris lifted me up in the air with my back pressed against the wall and my legs over his shoulders. He ate my pussy like imported dessert from France.

"Ouuuu," I moaned.

He slurped on me, almost making my soul float around the room in a celestial orgasm. Osiris rocked my body in ways I never thought was earthly possible. Back before all of this happened, I never assumed any of it would be happening. I figured he would remain just a familiar face in passing and not some man that swept me off my feet and intoxicated me with his presence. Although I never opened my mouth to tell him, I felt incomplete whenever he left for a day at a time. I wanted to be near him. He made me feel safe in ways I never felt safe before.

"You taste good, bae." Osiris got a gust of air before going back down to eat me out like he was at a five-star restaurant eating the most expensive item they served.

"Siris." I placed my hands on top of his head as my head drifted back against the wall. My entire body was weak from the way his tongue twirled against my clit. The way he moved up and went down as he aimed to please me in the worse way. All the pieces to my life slowly came together. Even if it only lasted for a short while, I was busy absorbing it all in the moment. "Fuck, ouuuu. Fuck!" He kept at what he was doing until I exploded into a million pieces in his mouth.

* * *

OSIRIS WALKED AHEAD of me with Axe behind me. I still wasn't fond of that nigga. He couldn't do his job the first time, so I couldn't stomach the fact that he was still on the team. He should've jumped his big ass in front of the bullet and my pop would've still been alive. I just prayed that if somebody tried to off me that one of my men jumped in the way of the gunfire to protect me.

"He all for show I see," I said. Wayne had the nicest cars parked out front, obviously flashing his wealth around. No matter how much money my pop brought in, he barely made it public by blowing it on cars and shit like that. He liked having a fat ass bank account compared to spending it on all assets to people please.

"Yeah, most of them are," Osiris said.

There were two men standing at the entrance. Osiris passed a few words with them before he pointed back to me and Axe. Then he turned around and passed a few more words. They stepped aside and let us in after chopping it up with Osiris for five minutes. When we were inside, the expensive shit kind of jumped out at me.

"They just let us in like that?" I looked around the building in question. What kind of nigga was Wayne to let a rival gang in his place without someone escorting them? I had to take a second look to see if we were being set up or not. Osiris wasn't in favor of meeting with Wayne at his HQ, but I told him we should go, so he followed my lead for a change. We had men on standby anyway if some shit popped off. Had them all in the trees with snippers if they had to shoot a nigga down from long range.

"That's what it seems." Osiris's voice was a dead giveaway that he was on pins and needles. He had his guards up, ready to blast a nigga coming from any direction. He made sure we both had on bulletproof vests. I argued it wasn't going to help, because Pop was wearing one the day he was murdered and still died due to the bitch ass nigga shooting him in the neck.

"There they are." I saw a short, brown skin man walking down the stairs.

"You gave your people the day off or some shit?" Osiris said as his greeting.

"No, they're just busy. Just follow me right upstairs." Wayne turned back around and started back up the stairs. Osiris and I exchanged glances and we followed Wayne's lead. Osiris told me earlier in the day Wayne was the reason Gooch was murdered thirteen years ago. That Pop never wanted to do business with the Serge Gs, and that he would never trust somebody like Wayne.

Wayne stood beside his office door and held his arm out for us to enter before him, but Osiris told him straight up we don't turn our backs to our enemies. Wayne didn't argue with that decision, he calmly walked in the office first and we followed, leaving Axe outside the door because if something popped off out there, we would know.

"You are really a beautiful woman. Lyric, right?" Wayne handed me a glass of champagne. On a different day I would've turned the wine down, but I wanted to show him that there was trust between us, to some degree. At least get that in his mind.

"Thank you, and yes that's correct." I took a seat on the chair that sat to the left of the desk. I felt Osiris's eyes burning into the side of my face. I told him before we were on the way over that we would play all the cards before we just shut Wayne down like Pop did over the years.

"Can't say I ever received the privilege to meet a woman who runs such a powerful gang." Wayne crossed his legs with his eyes glued to the glass of champagne he gave to me.

"An empire," I corrected.

"The 211 Vipers broke their alliance with me because I wouldn't side with them on making a hit on Don. And I'm truly sorry for your loss. I really am. It's like no one wants to get alone. It's time for us to put all the bad blood aside and come together." Wayne sounded like a genuine man, but Osiris had already put me on game. He said Wayne would talk a big deal, but his words never had much meaning. He only told people what he thought they wanted to hear. "How do you think Don knew about Beatz? Since he became the leader of 211 Vipers a few weeks back, they've been following his direct orders. Then he and T-

Max strolled up in here telling me 'bout their plan to bring down Don. I'm too old to be starting beef like that, so I opted out and they cut alliance."

"How do we even know this is the truth? And why the fuck are you telling all of this anyway? Do you think this is alliance-worthy information or something?" Osiris refused to take a seat. He continued to stand during the meeting. Judging by the sound of his voice, I thought he would jump at Wayne and start a war. "Don told us how cutthroat you are. How you feed people what they want to hear and shit."

"If that's the case then why did Don believe my every word 'bout Beatz? It was indeed the truth. How do you think Don knew he was heading up that way to visit Lyric? Because he told me. Beatz told me that he was going to murder Lyric to hurt Don, then strike when he was weak." Wayne laid more information on us. All his words sounded so real. Like damn, if he really was sitting up there lying then he was surely a dangerous man that wasn't to be trusted. "I want to be in alliance with the Eastside Warriors and if I'm not mistaking, it's not you who call the shots; it's her." Wayne looked away from Osiris and turned his attention to me. During the entire meeting, it was only the three of us. Whoever Wayne's right hand was, wasn't present. He didn't have any kind of advisor with him during the meeting. I could only imagine how things worked at his place. I figured he was the only one that could speak on anything while his men flocked to him like lost puppies.

"Well, before any decision is made, it goes through the both of us then it goes to my team. I make sure that every decision is in favor of my team. That's how we've always operated," I replied. Sitting there talking to Wayne, I knew Pop was somewhere looking down at me smiling at the way I was handling things. Proud of the way I continued to keep myself together when an average person would've fallen apart. While I was busy making sure the gang was still on top, Momma was out getting funeral arrangements together. I wanted to be there with her every step of the way, but I couldn't. I had a job to do.

"I see." Wayne poured a glass of whiskey and down it quicker than I'd seen any person consume a glass of whiskey. Then he fired up a big cigar. I could tell by all the things he was doing, he was a bit uneasy. It was going to take more than words to get me to even consider his decision. "Like I said, I'm just trying to keep gang violence at a low. I don't want to be at war forever. You know it gets kind of old."

"How do I know you didn't set Pop up in the first place? You two never saw eye-to-eye. He never wanted to be in partnership with you. So, how the fuck I know you ain't the one that's behind his death?" I slammed my fists against the desk, damn near scaring my damn self. I was filled with so much rage still, and although I was doing a decent job disguising it, I lost it inside of that office. I needed Wayne to know that I wasn't the type of bitch to do all that small, smooth talking shit.

"What do you want me to do to prove to you that I mean no harm?" Wayne kept his composure, which was a passing grade in my book. I just wanted to see how long he was going to keep that act up before he tried to hash a plan to knock me off the map, too.

"Let's meet with the 211 Vipers on my stomping grounds," I suggested. I saw Osiris viewing me from the corner of my eye, while Wayne stayed silent for a moment. There was no better way than to get everybody in the same room. "Deal?"

"I don't think that's a promising idea for either of our safety," Wayne said.

"I agree." Osiris was in favor of Wayne's reply, which made my blood boil over twice. He was there to be my advisor and in the same sense not to go against any decision I made on our team's behalf. "It's not good being amongst two enemies."

"I just meant, 211 Vipers are the ones responsible for murdering Don, and I'm sure they will try to do the same to you if given the right opportunity. It was in fact, part of their plan," Wayne said.

"I said we will meet with them together. Take the offer or leave it." I stood from the chair and let myself out of the office. Osiris was my right hand and he had to learn that I called the shots. Besides, I wanted to see Beatz face-to-face to know why the fuck he felt the need to murder my pop and when the hell he was initiated into some bullshit gang.

BEATZ

"Murder On My Mind," by YNW Melly, blasted over the speakers as I made my way into the kitchen to grab a drink and find the fuckin' drugs everybody was on. I was searching for something that would numb the pain.

"That muthafuckin' Beatz." I turned around upon hearing Wayne from behind me. Two men occupied him while T-Max was the only nigga near me. My other men were in the living room enjoying the party.

"Oh, what's up?" I reached out to give Wayne dab then focused back on raiding his place of booze and some other shit.

"Just making sho you're enjoying yourself. You know the man that brought Don to his grave has to have a good time at my expense," Wayne said.

"Well, do you have something stronger than booze? Like, I need something that's gon' send me to space or some shit like that." I grabbed a fifth of Vodka from the cooler and popped it open like it was just part of my everyday routine.

"Fo' sho. John Brown has all the shit you need." Wayne looked at the man to his right. The tall, greasy, light-skinned nigga was the lighter version of Biggie. The slower, no rapping ass version of Biggie.

"Then hook me up, John Brown." I took a swig of the Vodka with every intention of getting fucked up.

"I don't think that's a good idea. You have a lot of work that has to be done back at HQ. Shipments and all that. You know?" T-Max said those words like I was going to follow. With everything at Wayne's expense, I was set to have a fucking ball for once in my life. Really let go and get fucked up.

"You worry too much. Let him enjoy." Wayne pat T-Max's shoulder. I brushed T-Max off and followed John Brown down to the basement to get fucked up for the first in my life. The lower part of Wayne's house was laid just like the rest. He had white and gray color scheme, with expensive art hanging on the wall. Judging by Wayne's appearance, I thought for sure Scarface would've been hanging somewhere. It was kind of a letdown to not see the iconic godfather nowhere in the house.

"Pop this in your mouth." John Brown handed me two pills that were pink and purple; some damn Tic-tacs. I accepted them without thinking about it much. I popped them in my mouth and swallowed it down with Vodka. "And you need something stronger than that Vodka too." He walked over to the small frig that rested to the far end of the basement. And when he came back, he was handing me a doubled Styrofoam cup filled with purple liquid.

"What the hell is that?" I asked. I went most of my life watching out for what I consumed from people, making sure nobody laced my drinks or tried to fuck me up in my food. But, there I was accepting shit from a stranger like some dumb ass nigga. For all I knew, John Brown was feeding me poison and I was soon going to die. Fall asleep and never wake my ass back up.

"It's Lean nigga," John Brown said.

"Okay." I saw niggas from my hood drink the shit like water on the block and nothing happened, so I decided to down it right behind the Vodka and Mollies.

When I made it back upstairs, I was barely able to feel my face. The air was blasting in the house, but I couldn't feel shit on my flesh. Everything in front of me was moving in slow motion and the music sounded screwed.

"There he is." Wayne hit me on the shoulder like he did T-Max earlier.

"Where's T-Max?" I looked around the room in search of T-Max. The music was so loud and the house so crowded, I couldn't think straight. I wasn't sure what the hell I was trying to think about anyway. The whole point of getting fucked up was for me not to think in the first place.

"He stepped out for a moment." Wayne kept a sly smirk on his face. The entire moment felt wrong. I thought I would fall into my grave at any moment.

"Stepped out?" I was too fucked up to dwell on the fact that T-Max left me in the house while my men were busy partying. Wasn't nobody watching my back like they were supposed to.

"Let's not worry 'bout him. I have two bad women upstairs waiting on you. We have to make this celebration worthwhile, right?" Wayne shoved the empty Henny bottle against John Brown's chest, already in route to the upper floor.

"Okay then." I staggered the entire way upstairs. It was by the grace of God I didn't miss a step and fall to my death. Wayne had left me in the dust, and I had to use my better judgment to see which way he went upstairs. I took a quick left and headed down to the last room in that direction. The lighting in the room was a relaxing red. Slow jams were playing while one woman was sliding up and down a pole and the other one was laying with her legs wide open playing with her clit. I couldn't feel anything on my body leading up to the room, but I felt my dick stand straight up at the sight in front of me. They weren't some average women either; they were fine as fuck like they walked straight out of a hip-hop video. It was the dream of almost every man to be in the room with two drop dead sexy women.

"They're all yours for tonight." Wayne popped up out of nowhere, almost scaring my soul back down to the first floor.

"Thank you," I slurred. Time he walked out the room, the woman who was on the pole walked over to me. She gave me deep kisses before dropping to her knees to please me. After she wrapped her lips around my pipe, my entire mind blacked out. The rest of the night was a pleasurable blur.

* * *

I woke the next day on the floor of my office; the sun blasting through the big, doubled frame window. I squinted my eyes from the sensitivity of the sun. My head felt heavy and it ached all the way down to my spine. I felt like I woke in hell. There were vomit spots across the floor and the room's air reeked of stale booze. My body smelled like somebody drug me through a muddle of pig's waste.

"Oh, fuck. Never again. Never again." I grabbed my phone off the desk to check the time. My eyes bucked at the date and time. According to my phone, it was two days after the wild ass night and six o'clock in the evening. "What the fuck?"

I walked out the office and took slow, consistent strides down the stairs. I never prayed so hard to bump into an elevator. My legs were weak and my body fatigued from a hangover that I slept off for two whole days. They left me in the office to turn into a corpse.

"Goddamn, what's that smell?" T-Max appeared out of nowhere. When he was in front of me, he placed his shirt over his nose. He viewed me like I was the most disgusting person that ever walked the earth and that's exactly how I felt. "I'm happy to see you up, but you need to wash ya ass. We have some things to discuss. I'll send somebody up to clean your office before the meeting."

"What happened?" I scanned the lobby for a moment. It was quieter than normal. Like I didn't hear a damn thing. Not the sign of work being done. "What's going on?"

"What didn't happen? You went off the deep end at the party. Taking all kind of drugs and drinking wayyyy out of your league. You didn't want to listen to me, so I just stepped my ass back and gave you some space. I regret it now, though. I thought you were going to die up there," T-Max spoke with his mouth and nose still behind his shirt. I did smell. I had to clean up right after I finished up with T-Max. The good thing about HQ, there were smaller rooms on the lower floors designed like mini apartments.

"What do we have to discuss?" I placed my hands on my head. It pained me to speak. I just wanted to lay down, fall into a slumber again, forget the party even happened, and get my life back on track.

"The Eastside Warriors and the Serge Gs are having a meeting and we're invited. But there's a lot more we need to discuss," T-Max said.

"I see," I replied. Meeting with Wayne was no big deal. We were on good terms and he was pleased with my work and my team. Even when I stepped up to take the 211s from under his wings, we were still in alliance. We were good. However, the Eastside Warriors were after my blood after what happened to Don. It was in self-defense; nobody saw it that way, though. They were looking at me as a murderer; something that I viewed myself as. I pulled the trigger and shot to kill. Seeing Lyric after what happened wasn't in any favor of mine. I couldn't face her after my name was buzzing around the streets as the nigga who murdered Mr. Don. "Why the meeting though?"

"Something 'bout the gangs are ready to put an end to the violence." T-Max removed the shirt from his nose. "Look, just go wash up and meet me in my office. Not your office, but my office."

"Alright," I said and went on my way to get fresh. Lyric was still on my brain, though. She probably was going to have one of her men drop me time I stepped foot in their presence. It all could've been one big ass setup to murder me. To get Don's revenge. I wanted to see her though, because even with all the chaos in front of us, she was still the woman I loved without limits. The same girl that was my friend as a child. My best friend.

OSIRIS

I sat in the living room with Tara browsing the channels. I was in no mood to watch TV. I just attempted to act normal. I browsed through the same channels three times before I grew tired and turned off the TV. Tara was too busy on her phone to notice anything. That's how it had been since she made it back home. She was busy texting or whatever the fuck she was doing. While Oisin was too busy in everybody's business trying to get people to make better for themselves and leave the hood like there was a quick one-way ticket out without some hard ass work. Then I, on the other hand, was still juggling both places; home and HQ. Popping up on Brier during Don's funeral arrangements and all of that. She wanted it to be perfect. For it to go down in history on Don's behalf. A man like him had to be celebrated, even in death. He was ruthless with a heart of gold towards the hood. He wanted less violence in the streets and that's what Eastside had become over the years. People looked out for each other in those parts because of Don. It was him who made everybody on the block one big family.

"I think we should sell the house and leave this town behind." Tara peeped up from her iPhone's screen. Last I checked, I was the one helping Mom Duke out every step of the way and what happened to the house should've been my decision to make.

"I don't believe that's your decision to make though." I leaned back on the couch.

"It's all of our decision. I mean, receiving a little money off this house won't hurt us. And you can use the clean slate," Tara said. I knew Mom Duke was in a terrible situation and was facing death at any given moment, but I was still ready for Tara and Oisin to go back to where they came from. They were too damn worried about me. About my life and the path I was on. They had bread, however, I was sure that I was rolling in more dough than what they came across in one full year, regardless of the good jobs they had or career paths they chose.

"What is it with you and Oisin? Y'all think it's okay to force people to see life y'all way? This house, my life has nothing to do with either of you. Understand that?" I kept my composure. It wasn't the right time to snap on anybody. They couldn't sell the house without my permission and wasn't able to kick me out either if I decided to stay.

"We're only trying to look out for you, Siris. Damn, can't we do that as your older siblings?" Tara shook her head in disappointment. Right after she closed her mouth, there was a knock on the door, and I was the first to stand to answer it. With Mom Duke being terminally ill, there were a lot of people in and out of the house to visit her. Some even stayed until the end of the day. Her friends sometimes came over to play cards in room. It was good to see how so many people cared about her in her last days of life.

I swung the door open only to face the one woman I thought fell off the face of the earth. The one woman that I used to kind of love. Imani stood on the porch with a baby wrapped in a blanket.

"You just gon' stand and look at me or let us inside?" Imani said.

Her being pregnant by me was supposed to be a rumor. Nothing but talk the block didn't know a damn thing about. Rumors were spread all the time, only for them to be shut down the next week. Then the block would find the next big topic to discuss amongst themselves.

"What are you doing here?" I was waiting for the cameras to pop out and for somebody to tell me it was all a joke. I didn't need all that kind of drama in my life. Imani had been gone for at least a year. She fell off the face of the earth, then there she stood on the porch.

"I heard Ms. Vi is sick and don't have long to live so I thought it was only right to let her see her grandson." Imani rolled her eyes with every word. I was dealing with Mom Duke's illness, Don's death, being there for Lyric and her family through the whole thing, then Imani was standing on my porch with my *supposed* son.

"How do I know he's even mine?" She just popped up and placed more worry and stress on a nigga. If the lil' man really was my son, I had to really do all there was in my power to protect him and Imani.

"You don't know for sure, but I do. We can make a blood test appointment. I know he's your son Osiris, because you were the only nigga I was messing with. And hadn't messed with nobody else since. That's on my dead grandma," Imani said. I never known her to be the kind of woman to make up lies. When we were together, I believed she was only seeing me. It's not like she had much room to do anything else when we were together.

"Fuck." I took a deep breath. I looked around once more, trying to see if anybody would pop out and laugh at me for believing the joke, but no one ever did. "Fine. Come inside." Explaining a possible child to my family was easy. It was going to be a challenge with Lyric, though. She was young and already dealing with enough. Most young women didn't do the whole nigga with a kid thing, due to the amount of drama that sometimes came along with the baby's mom.

"Who was it at the door," Tara asked when I made it back into the living room. She looked at me then back at Imani. "Who is that?"

"That's Imani and that baby she is holding might be my child; my son." I introduced the two of them. During my brief relationship with Imani, she had the pleasure of meeting my Mom Duke once and Jab a handful of times. We weren't as serious as she thought, so I saw no need in getting her used to any aspect of my family. Plus, my family got attached to be people quick, especially Mom Duke. She called everybody on the block her daughter or some shit like that. She opened her house up for a lot of people over the years too, back when we were younger. She really was like the mother of the neighborhood.

"Child?" Tara questioned. My personal life was top secret. I never picked up the phone to talk to my siblings about anything. Hell, we barely even talked on the phone. And whenever we did, I allowed them to shower me with their accomplishments while I congratulated them every time. I was proud of them, even when I knew they would never be proud of me.

"Yeah." I took a seat back on the couch. The last thing I wanted to be was a deadbeat dad, so I was going to be there for my child. If I knew for sure he was mine, I would've even signed the birth certificate, and showered him with expensive gifts. I would've never forced Imani to go through the pregnancy alone. When I heard she was pregnant, it was by word of mouth. I tried calling her a few times, but she never answered any of my calls. So, I let it go and ruled it as another rumor on the streets.

"Oh my god. Let me hold him. Go get Momma, Siris." Tara had a soft spot for children ever since I could remember. She used to take me everywhere with her back in the day. I used to kick it with her and her friends when I was a young nigga. Listening to all their girl talk and shit, which made me grow up to trust women a little less. All the shit they did with other niggas while in a relationship would make any boy grow up to have trust issues.

As I left the living room to get Mom Duke, I overheard Tara telling Imani how much the child looked like me as a baby. I ignored her and kept on my way to Mom Duke's room. Just in case the baby was mine, I wanted Mom Duke to meet her grandson.

BANG. BANG. BANG. BANG.

"Yo Ma, can I come in real quick?" I said from behind the door.

"Just break the door off the hinges then boy." Mom Duke complained in her whisper of a voice. It was like each day her voice became more unrecognizable. It pained me every time I heard her speak. Just a few weeks back she was able to talk without wanting to sleep, and she was able to hold a conversation with me like old times. "Come on in."

I turned the doorknob and let myself in the room. She'd been in that room for days, just suffering in bed. I don't even think she attempted to get out of bed at all.

"I have somebody that wants to meet you," I said as I approached the bed.

"Somebody to meet me? It better not be no man either. I can't do nothing with a man on my deathbed. All I'll be able to do is look at his dick. I can't do nothing like that." Mom Duke rambled on about nonsense. She should've known I was the last person to bring a man in the house for her. I couldn't stand a man being next to Mom Duke. She was always too good in my eyes for any man.

"No. It's your grandson," I said.

"Grandson?" Mom Duke questioned.

"Yeah. You remember Imani? Well, she was pregnant by me and had a baby a few months ago. A baby boy." I should've added *supposedly* at the end of that sentence. Mom Duke deserved good news on her deathbed.

"Boy, why you kept me in the dark on something like this? I ain't even buy the child nothing. You should be ashamed of yourself. Get out my room." Mom Duke slung her cover to the floor to get out the bed like she was given a boost of energy. "Get out!"

"Ma, I know and I'm sorry. I can't just let you get out of bed by yourself." I backed away from the bed with my hands in the air to show her I didn't mean any harm.

"I got this, just get your ass outta here before I beat you with my belt," Mom Duke fussed.

I listened to her demands and I removed my ass out of her room. She wasn't about to beat me for old time's sake.

* * *

While everybody was in the house showering the baby with love, I was on the porch with Jab smoking a big blunt. Out of everybody in the family, Jab understood why I wasn't in there pretending and shit. I needed concrete evidence before I got involved. I refused to get attached to the child only for the test results to come back and slap me in the face with news I wasn't in favor of.

"When they laying Don to rest?" Jab asked while he focused on preparing another blunt since I was busy hogging the one he brought over to share.

"Brier still in the process of making arrangements. She's really set on making sure he goes out with a bang. I can't blame her either. Don did a lot for her, their family and the town. He deserves the best." I took a drag of the blunt until my lungs couldn't pull anymore smoke.

"I still can't believe the shit happened, though. Like, I really thought the OG was untouchable." Jab focused on breaking the weed up, but then he paused for a moment and finally said, "You need to get out, Siris. Like I mean, start over. You don't have to be a part of that gang forever."

"Nope. No. Don't even start with me 'bout that. You of all people know better. We already talked about this." I nipped that conversation in the ass before it went any farther. Jab already knew my feelings about the entire situation. He knew it was more than just being part of a gang. The Eastside Warriors had my loyalty. I swore to Don that I would watch out for Lyric with my last breath. I was a man of my word and wasn't going to break it now because Don wasn't there to hold me to them.

"I'm just saying, bruh. You can be there for Lyric without you two being part of the gang. And last I checked, that's not the life she wants for herself anyway. Isn't her dream to be a rapper?" Jab still stayed on topic after I shut him down about everything. To me, it sounded like he'd been doing some talking with Tara and Oisin, which made my temples throb.

"You being like that now bruh? Like, you seriously telling me what's best? I thought we were better than that. Better than trying to push each other's way of life on one another? I don't even feel like kicking it with you anymore." I got up from the rocker and left Jab on the porch alone to break up his weed. Being in the midst of my family drained my soul. It seemed like every corner I turned, somebody was trying to preach to me. It was ten times worse than before since Don was dead. I guess they were afraid I was going to die by the streets, too. If I did, at least it meant I died as a real ass nigga out there. Don was a legend out there when he was alive and the muthafuckin' G.O.A.T since he was dead. It was going to be a whole lot of young niggas following in his shoes now. You weren't a real OG until you were dead.

Mom Duke was sleep on the couch with the baby while Tara, Imani and Oisin was busy having what seemed like a good conversation. I headed into the kitchen to grab my car keys. We had a lot of shit going on within the gang that I had to get back to.

"I'm heading out. Tell Mom Duke I'll be back tomorrow." I headed to the door on a mission to get the hell out of there quick as I could before Tara and Oisin decided to try to talk what they called *sense* into me.

"You're not going to hold your son? He looks just like you," Oisin said.

"I have to head out. Just let Mom Duke know I'll be back." I continued on my path out the door without looking back or trying to defend myself. I wasn't sure the child belonged to me and I wasn't going to step up until proven otherwise.

LEX

"Where are you going?" Lyric walked behind me like a concerned mother. I didn't like that new side of her; the side that was extra protective. I understood all the risk of me going somewhere alone, but I couldn't sit up there in that building forever and allow my life to past me by. She was doing what she thought was right by Pop while I was struggling to figure out what the hell I was doing in the first place.

"Back up off me, Lyric. I need to go someplace to breathe," I fussed.

"Go someplace alone like the last time. You think you that slick that nobody saw you out in town a few nights ago. What the fuck were you doing on the Southside anyway when we have enemies over there?" Lyric grabbed my arm, forcing me to turn around. She was my older sister and I respected her to a certain point. She was riding my back, doing shit Momma wasn't even doing.

"Stop sweating me, okay. I'm dealing with all this the best I know how. Now let go of my fuckin' arm," I said through clenched teeth. She was really bugging that day. I wasn't even planning on getting in any trouble. I wanted to make a stop by Mr. Griffin's house to see how he was doing and to get word on Michael's funeral. I couldn't miss saying my final goodbyes to him.

"But being reckless isn't dealing with anything; it's just causing more problems. Don't you see that? They could've kidnapped you and did God knows what to you." Lyric finally released my arm.

"Lyric, go crawl back under Osiris and leave me alone. At least I'm dealing with my grief in other ways than getting under a man to please me." I turned away from her and continued on my way outside of the building.

"You ain't taking his truck again. If you gon' go somewhere then you best find a way to go since you so grown now." Everything in my body was telling me to knock Lyric in the mouth. She had no right telling me I couldn't use the truck. She didn't own a damn thing but the position that she fell into. And if anybody was really observing either of us, I deserved the spot more. I had more heart than Lyric when it came down to the streets. She was too damn soft; didn't even know how to shoot a gun because she was so afraid to let Pop teach her. It was crazy how Pop and I had our bitter moments when we were so much alike. I guess that's why we never clicked to begin with.

"Try to stop me, bitch." I continued my route to the track. If she wanted to take the keys from me, she was going to have to beat my ass and take them or have one of her men to put me down.

"Lex, just stop it. I know you're hurting. I'm hurting too. But what you're doing isn't going to make things better." Lyric's voice sounded distant. When I turned around once I was at the truck, she was standing near the front of the building with her hands resting on her hips. There was a thing or two she had to learn about me: when my mind was made up, that was the end of the story.

I hopped in the truck and headed on my merry way out of the gates. The worse thing that could happen on my way to the Eastside was being stopped by the cops, only to be asked for a license I didn't have. But if the right cops stopped me, they were going to let me go once they found out who I was. My pop's name wasn't just big on the streets; it was huge amongst people in higher positions, too.

That day I had one thing in mind, and that was to visit Mr. Griffin. I knew Lyric would've understood had I told her the truth instead of giving her a tough time. I wanted to show her that she didn't run things the way she thought and that I wasn't one of the niggas who swore their loyalty to the gang.

My phone started going off when I reached the turnoff to the main road that led back to town. The woods out there was a bit tricky. Sometimes it surprised me that we even had cell phone signal.

"Hello?" I answered.

"Lex?" Beatz voice blared from the speakerphone. I held my words in for a moment, trying to think about why the fuck he was on my phone or why the fuck he even thought it was okay to call me. "Please don't hang up. This is important."

"I'm listening," I replied, trying to stay focused on the task at hand. Driving on the Holly road was dangerous when a person wasn't paying attention. Too many head on collisions happened over the years according to the older people.

"I didn't mean to murder Don. I thought about it on a few occasions, but that was it. He pulled up and started emptying fire. Lex, I ain't want to die, so I started firing back." Beatz sounded tore up, as if he'd been hit upside the head with a brick and was just waking up days later. "I never meant to hurt Lyric, you, or nobody for that matter. To be honest, I don't even know what possessed me to be part of this bullshit anyway."

I remained quiet as I tried to process his every word. His words didn't mean much and I hated myself for listening to what he had to say. If what he was saying was indeed the truth, then I felt sorry for him for having to be in that situation. However, he was grown; he made that mess for himself. He knew what kind of monster he was dealing with when he poked it awake.

"I didn't mean for Michael to get killed that day. Everything went left. It just happened. I never meant for any of it to happen," Beatz said with a slight break in his tone like he was sobbing. I was aware he was behind Pop being killed; he was the one who pulled the trigger. I was dealing with that in my own way. However, to know that he was behind Michael's shooting too turned me into a rage. I was in desperate need to strangle him.

"You didn't mean? That's all I'm hearing. No apology or anything. It's you didn't fucking mean. It happened Beatz. They're both dead because of you." I had to let up on the gas because I had the pedal to the metal like my life was depending on it. "Save that stupid ass shit for somebody else." I ended the call with instant regret traveling to my temples. I needed to say more. I wanted him to know what he did would never be forgiven by any of us. For him to live with the two lives on his conscience until he died. So, I dialed the number back praying he picked up. He had to hear what the fuck I had to say.

"Now you listen to me," I said. What he was about to hear was probably going to send him into a lake of tears, or even make him commit suicide. Whatever he did after the call was on him. "You lost Lyric, you lost your life; your dreams. You will be living in fear until they kill you. You will be an outcast to the people you grew up with. You've made yourself an enemy to the Eastside. What you did will never be forgiven by anybody." I ended the call and that time I was pleased with what I told him. I prayed he felt every word to the core of his stomach and that those very words kept him up at night. For the longest, I'd known Beatz. He never hung out around bad company or got into any trouble, so when I found out he was the one to murder Pop it surprised me. Then to know he was the one who was behind Michael's murder brought me to tears.

* * *

Like usual, Mr. Griffin's house was empty. Not even after Michael's death was the driveway packed with cars. Not like ours would've been if our house would've never been burned to the foundation. All our memories were gone. Some of them I was happy that they perished within the fire. All the days Pop tossed Momma against the wall, tossed pots across the kitchen only to stain the floors and she had to clean up like a maid. All the days my anxiety invited itself in my bed only to wrap its hands around my throat and take me under an ocean.

I hopped out the car, quickly making my way up the driveway so nobody would spot me. People were always hanging, shooting dice, and playing card. Plus, it was summer, so the streets were packed. I made it to the door without anybody noticing me. I gave the door a few knocks before Mr. Griffin approached it.

"What do you want?" Mr. Griffin said through the crack of the door.

"I just wanted to give my condolences for your loss. I know you're going through a hard time right now." My stomach pained from anxiety and my heart raced. I just wanted the moment to be over already. Like be completely over.

"Well, that's very thoughtful of you considering he lost his life protecting you from your dad's enemies. And I think Allah has a funny way of dealing with people," Mr. Griffin spoke ill to me. It almost sounded like he blamed me for Michael's death, but I was innocent too. I had nothing to do with the gang or any of that. Since Michael was murdered, I was blaming everybody except myself.

"Mr. Griffin, I-I never meant him any harm. I didn't know those men were driving up on the block to kill somebody. I'm sorry you feel that way about me, about my family or the fact you're relieved my pop is dead." Tears welled in my eyes and I couldn't hold them in. I was a wreck at that front door. Mr. Griffin sure chose his words wisely to make me feel low. To make me feel like I was the one who pulled the trigger on Michael.

I stepped away from the door with my head down. Anger road my back like a monkey. Picturing myself bashing his mouth in made me feel a whole lot better. He hadn't ever been fond of me or my family. He used to make smart-ass remarks about the Eastside Warriors and how gang leaders were corrupting the youth. I agreed with him to some degree, but for him to really say all that in front of me, knowing my pop's background, wasn't necessary. If I would've went toe-to-toe with him and let him know how Michael was ready to move away whenever he turned eighteen, he would've been the one in tears like a punk ass bitch.

"Yooo Lex, come'mere real quick. Let me holla at you." Qbaby was like three years older than me. He kept a low profile, although he lived by the streets and the code of the Eastside Warriors. I even heard he tried to get on the team. He failed too many initiations though, and Pop wrote him off as a lost cause. I had every intention to speak with Mr. Griffin and go kick it with Moomoo before it got too late and her grandma started tripping.

I quickly wiped my eyes as I headed to the house next door. "Meet me right here." I was standing in the driveway waiting for Qbaby. There was no way I was about to walk on that porch in the company of all those older niggas.

When Qbaby reached me, the first thing he did was hug me. I'm not talking about some sideways hug or bodies poked away from each other type of hug. He was pressed all against me, holding me tight as fuck. It felt good, like I needed that kind of love from somebody, but I quickly pushed away.

"What's up?" I asked.

"I'm sorry for what happened to your dad. He was a good man and a lot of people respected him. I just can't believe some pussy ass nigga would down him like that." Qbaby said those words with a whole lot of hurt in his eyes. I wouldn't have been surprised to know that the entire hood was in mourning about Pop. That his death made people forget about Michael being gunned down in the streets just a day before. It was crazy out there. And what really surprised me was that Qbaby didn't even know Beatz was the one to pull the trigger on Pop, which meant the hood didn't know he was an enemy.

"Yeah, thank you. It means a lot," I replied. For the most part, I'd been keeping my emotions in check with the help of a little weed here and there.

"No prob. And if you want to, you can come kick it with me and my crew sometimes. We 'on be doing nothing but blazing, drinking a lil' bit and you know, playing dice and shit like that. Ain't nothing too wild be going on." Qbaby flashed me with his two rows of gold teeth, and those dimples in his jaws were beautiful. I don't think I ever used that word on a boy until then. And the way the sun kissed his flesh made him ten times more attractive. I had a serious weakness for chocolate niggas.

"I don't know. It's a bunch of old niggas in your circle. I'm not trying to be a victim." I was kindly declining Qbaby's offer to hang out with his crew. I never knew them to mess around with young girls or harm anybody. My pop was dead though, and wasn't no telling who wanted to harm us now because they could.

"It's not even like that. I mean, I want to kick it with you in a different way if that's cool. My niggas know how to behave themselves." Qbaby viewed me from my waist all the way back to my face. The block had definitely changed, and my pop's death made niggas bolder because if he was still alive, there was no way I would've been standing in that driveway almost drooling over Qbaby like that. "Just lock my number in your phone if you change your mind and you give me your number."

"Okay." I let that word slip out my mouth way too easy. If Lyric taught me anything concerning boys, she told me to always play hard to get. Make them work for anything having to do with me. Give a little attitude because niggas like that. They complained about females being mad rude, but they were low key in love with it though. I broke the code and surrendered too quick.

"Cool. Cool. Here lock it in here." Qbaby handed me his phone and accepted mine. Once we locked each other's number in the phones, we exchanged phones again. "If I don't hear from you. You will definitely be hearing from me."

"Alright, bet." I removed myself from the driveway and headed back to the SUV that I parked in Mr. Griffin's driveway; the arrogant Muslim nigga who turned his nose up at everybody who wasn't in the same faith as him. He gave the faith a bad a rep, which needed to be addressed by whoever his leader was.

* * *

Moomoo was on the porch peeling peas with Ms. Gale. She was like the only person I knew who still peeled peas faithfully and didn't purchase them from the grocery store According to Moomoo, there was a whole lot of other old habits her grandma had. Like not using lights at night and lighting candles instead. She didn't like Moomoo to turn the air conditioner on in the summer either. I couldn't imagine living like that. It was a good sight though; them enjoying each other's company, even with Moomoo looking like she wanted to be rescued.

"Hey Ms. Gale. Moomoo," I greeted.

"Hey baby," Ms. Gale spoke with the thickest Louisiana accent. We were all down bad country, but I was sure Ms. Gale had us all beat on the block. She showered herself in the accent and loved when somebody asked to hear her speak. "I'm sorry 'bout what happened to Don. He was good folk out this way. Nobody had to approve of his way of life to like him. He ain't did no harm to me. How ya momma 'em doin'?"

"Grandma." Moomoo shook her head.

"What I say wrong na, gal?" Ms. Gale asked.

"No, it's fine. You ain't say nothing wrong Ms. Gale." I took a seat on the porch railing. I'd gone through the craziest range of emotions that day, from dealing with Lyric, to getting talked down on by Mr. Griffin and feeling a bit of relief being in Qbaby's good grace. He wasn't any known nigga on the block; I just knew he was good people. "And thank you. Momma holding up while Lyric, I don't really know. Boni don't know what's really going on, though."

"It troubles to me to know that we as a people went to being killed down by white folks, only to shoot each other down in the streets." Ms. Gale peeled her last pea haul. She grabbed her big silver pot and headed to the door. Before she went inside, she turned to look at me, "If you need anything just let me know."

"Yes ma'am," I replied. Once Ms. Gale was long gone inside of the house, I went to filling Moomoo in about Qbaby, only to take my mind off my true feelings of what I was facing alone, basically. Nobody really understood me; and the one person who did was dead.

LYRIC

"You trying to go over there to the Southside?" Osiris walked in the building frantic. Somebody in the gang had to have snitched on me to Osiris. Because I know I wasn't the one to tell him about my plans to ride out over to the Southside to meet with Beatz since he failed to show at the meeting we had with the Serge Gs.

"You worrying 'bout what the fuck I'm doing when nobody brought that nigga to me yet." I went off right back at him. He was talking all that big shit like he was going to have Beatz by the ears, but when that plan failed, I decided to try and lure him in to get his side of the story and possibly have somebody to murder his ass.

"You said you wanted him alive. You never gave the orders for us to get the nigga, so don't start with me on that shit." Osiris shut my argument down and focused on what the fuck I had going.

"Which one of these niggas called you?" I folded my arms as I viewed Osiris from across the room. He had it bad snapping at me when he was in a rage. The niggas was doing way too much.

"It don't matter which nigga informed me. I just know what you not 'bout to do out there. If you want the nigga here in your keeping, then

I'll make sure he gets here." Osiris was typing at the speed of lightning on his phone. "And all you slumped over, African jungle lookin' niggas get to work. Don't be standing around looking at me and shit. Got me fucked up." The few men that occupied the lobby scattered like schoolchildren; all I was able to do was roll my damn eyes at them. They were more afraid of Osiris than me, when I was the one who really called all the shots. Shit had to drastically change if I was going to oversee the gang for real. They had to take me serious and learn not to overstep my rules by calling Osiris down on me. What I said was supposed to go.

"You need to calm your attitude." I shook my head at how Osiris came at me sideways. I knew he was dealing with a lot of shit. We both were. He had to check his temper though, and stop throwing fits every chance he received.

"Head upstairs, I need to speak with you in private." Osiris past by me without a hug or a warm greeting. He walked in the building already on ten, now he was bossing me around like I was ranked underneath him. I wasn't sure how to feel about any of it. He had me for the wrong bitch. My attitude was cruel, too. I was crazy when I wanted shit to go my way or no way. That's how it was.

By the time I made it upstairs, he was already in the office sitting behind the desk in my chair instead of sitting where he was supposed to sit. "That's how we doing shit now?"

"Is this what you really want for your life?" Osiris asked.

"What do you mean?" I shot him a question back. Downstairs we were talking about the stupid decision I made and how some niggas ratted me out to him, now he flipped the entire topic and turned it on me and what I truly wanted out of life. If I wasn't mistaken, I thought I went over that went him. I told him I was stepping up to uphold my pop's name. It's how it was always supposed to happen. Plus, I wanted to live knowing my pop was proud looking down at me.

"Like, do you really want this for your life? I know you was into music and all that. You had this big dream to escape this life. So, I need to know if this is what you truly want for yourself, or if you're just doing it because you know this is what Don wanted?" Osiris stared me dead in the soul. I looked away from him for a moment, then brought my attention back to his handsome ass face.

"This how it has to be," I replied.

"Lyric, if this not the life you want then you need to run away now before you get too caught up in this shit. If you really want to be this big star, you need to move away and go for it." Osiris propped his elbows on the desk. "I don't want you to stay in this gang because I want to be next to you always. I refuse to make you stay in something you'll regret a few years down the road." I swear it was like Osiris was reading my soul, like he had a device in my brain and was reading my every thought. I hadn't mentioned it to nobody, but I had my second thoughts about everything. I kept thinking about me having children, only for me to be shot dead in the streets and the cycle repeating itself. It was a challenging thing to think about when Pop had so much faith in me before he took his last breath. He placed that shit on my shoulders and it was heavy as fuck to carry. It felt weird not knowing much about anything dealing with the streets and holding a position as a honcho. It was fuckin' crazy. I felt like if that was really what he wanted me to do, then he should've groomed me for it ahead of time.

"Siris, I have no choice. I can't fold on the team now. My momma, Lex, Boni, and the entire Eastside is depending on me. I can't run from this shit. All those fancy dreams are gone. They have to wait until I figure this all out." I wasn't prepared to have a serious conversation regarding my choice. I wanted to fold; to pack my shit and run for the hills and be free. It's the logical thing we should've done since Pop was no longer with us. We were playing a dangerous game and didn't know if there were any more enemies planning to strike.

"You have a choice, Lyric. You do." Osiris kept pushing me to throw in the towel. I couldn't understand why he had a change of heart.

"Why are you trying to get rid of me? What's going on?" I poked around for some answers. He was far too aggressive with his approach about me choosing the right path. He tried his hardest to get in my conscience. "What the fuck is going on?"

"It's just." Osiris took a deep breath. His eyes were fixed on me like he was about to lay the worse kind of news on me. "I have a lot going on, and there's a lot going on out in the streets. I just don't want you to get caught up in something you're going to regret."

"Osiris, what's really going on?" I asked the question again for the second time. He took his own time to answer me. He needed to speak the fuck up and let me in on what was going on so I wouldn't feel like I was in the dark.

"Well, the truth is, one of my old girls showed up at my Mom Duke's house and told me I have a son. He's only a few months old." Osiris looked into my eyes when he laid that news on me.

"You ain't know until now? Like, you dropped her like that while she was pregnant?" I stood from the chair and paced the room. My stomach ached with anger.

"Lyric, I'm not even sure if it's mine or not. We still have to get the DNA test done, the results have to come back and all of that." Osiris tried make it seemed like it was wasn't a big deal; like him having a son wasn't a big deal. I just felt some kind of way about him leaving the child's mother for over nine months without giving a helping hand. "My brother and sister has been on my ass 'bout changing my life around, and I thought 'bout it too. Like, if this ain't what you want, I can give this all up."

"What about the oath you made to the team and the promise to my pop?" With the news Osiris laid on me, I was in no favor to just leave it all behind and run. He had a possible child living in the state, and hopping across the country with me meant he was going to be leaving his son behind. "Then you can't just leave your son. Because you know if we just drop all of this, we won't be safe out here anymore."

"I'm willing to do all that for you lil' shawty. As long as Don lived, I upheld my oath to him. It's all about you now. What do you want?" Osiris said.

"We're going to ride this all out." I wasn't going to throw in the towel. We were going to thrive as the leading faces amongst the Eastside Warriors, continuing the legacy my pop started.

"Aight, word. But for now, I want you to focus on Don's funeral. Grieve as much as you need to while I bring an end to our enemies." Osiris was a man of his word. When he told me he would put an end to all the bullshit, I knew he would. There was no doubt in my mind that the two 211 Vipers were going to feel the wrath and my stilettos were going to be in Beatz's neck.

* * *

"Glory, glory, hallelujah, when I lay my burdens down," the choir sang. The entire morning it felt like I was suffocating; like the air was so toxic I could barely breathe. It was all real. Pop was dead and his funeral was beating me down to my knees. Last time I was at a funeral was for Mall, and during the entire service, Pop was there to help me get through it. My entire body was weak and my chest was on fire from the sorrow I tried my best to keep inside. I'd cried since the day Pop was shot. I'd beaten myself up about it for an entire week. Then the closer it got to his funeral, the dreams started. The shooting that resulted in his death blasted in my ears and woke me up like I was reliving it all.

"Thank you, choir." Pastor Roy stood behind the pulpit with his handkerchief and his bible already open. My heart was racing in my chest. Everything was moving too damn fast. One minute the choir was singing then the next, Pastor Roy was about to give a sermon. His face was already washed down in sweat and he hadn't even started.

"Can I get an amen?" Pastor Roy said.

"Amen. Hallelujah," the church crowd said in unison. Momma told me throughout the week that she wanted Pop to go out in the best way possible. She refused to just have a funeral where people say a few words on his behalf, then it was time to put him in the ground. She wanted a full service like the church had on Sundays.

"The Lord said after this life, to dust a man shall return right?" Pastor Roy said.

"Yes Lord." I heard a few shouts from the back row.

"To dust a man shall return. We can, we can have all the material things in the world. All of it. And none of it stops us from returning to dust." Pastor Roy flipped through a few pages in the bible as he wiped his sweaty forehead for the second time. "That is, unless a person, like these rich folks out there in Hollywood, get their bodies preserved." There were a few laughs in the church. I guess he intended for his last words to contain a bit of humor because even he cracked a smile. I couldn't find anything funny, though. I wanted to ball up on the seat and cry my heart out.

"I know it's a hard thing to think about; to leave family behind, but it's something we all have to do says the Lord in the book of Ecclesiastes 3:20: *all go unto one place; all are of the dust, and all will turn to dust again.*" Pastor Roy looked up from the bible. I don't why, but his eyes fell right to me. "As long as you live your life according this book and hold onto His words, death won't be such a scary thing. I know sometimes we get sucked in by our peers. We try to walk a clean path and they whisper in our ear, feeding us with their venom, and now we're on their path and off our own."

"I can't stay in here," I whispered.

Osiris grabbed my hands and held them tight. "It's okay, Lyric. It's okay." His words weren't as comforting as I hoped. I couldn't sit in that church for another minute; it was too damn much. The pastor's words were too much. All the shouts from people in the church was unbearable and the songs that the choir sung tore my spirit up. But above all, I felt convicted, like the entire sermon was directed towards me. It all brought me back to what Osiris asked me just a day ago. *Was I sure of my decision?* I stood from the seat, darted out the big, heavy mahogany doors and fell on my knees time the sunlight hit against my skin. But I wasn't prepared for what stared back at me from across the street.

BEATZ

I crossed the street without thinking about what would happen to me. I was way out of my league being there. I wasn't invited, and the entire Cotton family hated me with a violent hatred. I had to show my face, though. I snuck away from T-Max and my assigned guards to see Lyric.

"Get back, get back." I turned around only to see my nightmare to the left of me. Some man was aiming an AK-47 at me. I knew she was going to be surrounded by men who were willing to die. But see, I was willing to die just to be close to her. Everything that I did was for her and because of her. It was her fault that I was caught up in the streets. I blamed her for abandoning me time temptation stepped to her face.

"It's okay." Lyric stood from her knees and walked down the steps of the church. She was nothing like the last time I saw her. Her eyes were dark, and her complexion shadowed by grief. I had to give it to her; she was still the most beautiful girl that my eyes ever fell on.

Osiris stood right behind her with his hands folded in front of him like his hands was on a pistol in his tux pocket. Death didn't scare me anymore.

"Can you just hear me out," I said once she was standing right in front of me. She called her guards off, but they still had their guns on me. The Eastside Warriors treated enemies harsh and they were prepared to pop a cap in whoever. I couldn't stress it enough; I wasn't ever her enemy or Don's. I was an enemy to nobody at all. "Please."

"You have some muthafuckin' nerves showing up here. Are you out of your fuckin' mind? You want a bullet in your head, on your own terms, I see. You're the one who pulled the trigga, but shows up on his funeral day. Who the fuck has the balls to do some shit like that?" Lyric hit me so fast, it made my heart race. I thought somebody had shot me in the dome. "You murdered my pop and still want me to have some pity towards you. You want be all in my good grace and shit."

"Lyric, I believe somebody set me up." It was the first time I expressed those feelings to anybody since Don was dropped back at the hotel. Things weren't adding up. Like, I knew my orders went left and people did whatever they wanted. "It wasn't my intentions to kill Don. That morning I came up there to see you and only you. Not to have no kind of run-in with Mr. Don. The fire at the warehouse; that was my fault. The shooting of Michael was my fault because an innocent bullshit plan went left."

"So, you did all that shit, but you ain't mean to see him that day. To me, it all just followed your lil' plan. Just own up to your shit like a man." Lyric growled in my face with darkness layered in her eyes. It was a scary sight to see the purest woman turned rough. She wasn't going to be satisfied until somebody dropped me. "Get this nigga out of here."

"Wait Lyric, please. I'm trying to tell you." I pled for her to hear me out; to listen to me.

"Tell me that you've been bragging 'bout the shit? Talking to niggas in high power 'bout my pop being dead to make it one big joke. Nigga your time is up." Lyric walked past me and left me standing there in the middle of the lion's den. Osiris wanted me out the picture since day one. He couldn't live to see Lyric and I thrive. So, I knew he was eating all that shit up. I could've bet money on him rejoicing in my sudden downfall. I viewed the man to the left of me closing in and there was two men to the right closing in with Osiris meeting up in front of me. They trapped me. I dug my own grave that day. I don't know why I thought coming to Lyric would have her to call all her men off me. Like her seeing me would remind her of the love we once shared; of the love I still housed for her. If I somehow lived to see another day, lived beyond the chaos, there wasn't ever going to be another woman who took my heart like she'd done over the years. She was my all.

"You done bitch," I heard Osiris say. Everything went black after that.

*　*　*

"WAKE THAT PUSSY NIGGA UP." The voice was vicious. The sound of the evil that belonged to the voice troubled my soul. I just knew God sent my ass to hell. All the praying my momma did over the years didn't measure up to a damn thing. I was in hell. A lost cause that nobody was able to rescue. "You made the job so damn easy nigga. Where they make your kind at?"

"Wh-where am I?" I murmured as my eyes slowly opened to the bright light. The light was similar to the light the pastor used to preach about when I was a child in Sunday school. The bright light we see before God snatched our breath. If I wasn't in hell then I was surely dying.

"Nigga you in Warriors territory." The voice belonged to the one and only, Osiris. My biggest enemy that walked the earth. The nigga who stole my woman and turned her against me.

"Kill me already." My eyes wouldn't open any farther than a squint. Sudden pain traveled across the front of my head like somebody struck me with the heaviest object they were able to find. Going to see Lyric was a terrible idea. It landed me in the arms of her nigga, and in the den of my snakes. "Just get it over with."

"Ah, hell. You don't understand. There's no easy way out of this. You must pay for this until Lyric says your dues are paid in full," Osiris said. To know Lyric was behind the torture pained me. For her to even think I killed Don intentionally troubled the end of my spirit. "This how hoe niggas like you go out."

"Where's Lyric?" I couldn't care less about what Osiris had to say. I had to hear Lyric's voice to see if it was her who really ordered them to torture me that way. After I said those words, everything went black again.

OSIRIS

Lyric was standing in the hallway when I exited the room from with Beatz. I don't think nobody was expecting him to just show up like that. Hell, it surprised me that none of the niggas from his crew contacted us on his behalf. I know they figured the day would come when we got hands on him. But they weren't even trying to make a deal with the Eastside Warriors on the young, punk nigga's behalf.

"I think that's enough," Lyric said.

"Enough? That nigga murdered your dad. Don is gone because of him," I protested. No kind of punishment was good enough for the nigga. He deserved to be tortured until he died from the pain. "Nothing's enough, Lyric."

"Siris, I don't like this. I know what he did was horrible. I know. I just think we should go ahead and end it." Lyric walked away from me and let herself inside the room with Beatz. It rubbed me the wrong way to even think that she was trying to give the nigga some kind of mercy. There wasn't any need of her going in there in the first place. I had everything handled. He was suffering at my hand, per her orders.

"Lyric, don—" it was too late for me to stop her. The condition Beatz was in was going to make her heart bend towards him. She didn't need to see him like that.

"Oh my god. Siris, what have you done?" Lyric's hands flew to her mouth. I followed her orders. She wanted the nigga to feel my wrath, so that's what I made sure he felt with all the pain I inflicted on him. I kicked his ass so good. His eyes were swollen shut and I was sure he suffered from broken ribs. When he cried out for help, it triggered more anger out of me and I wanted him to suffer more. To feel the pain Don probably felt when he was shot. To feel what it was like to be close to death. I had every intention to make him suffer in my own way.

"I told you not to come in here. Didn't I tell you?" I grabbed Lyric's arm, trying my best to get her out of there before she went back on her orders.

"This isn't right. I can't do this." Lyric's voice trembled as she reached out to touch Beatz's unrecognizable face.

If she let him live, I don't think he was going to be able to look at himself in the mirror without wanting to end it. Back when Don taught me as a lil' nigga, he instilled in me the most gruesome ways to make somebody pay for their wrong. It was the way of the Eastside Warriors. It was our law to inflict that kind of pain. It was the law Lyric still had to grow used to. Because if she was going to be in the gang, leading all of us, she had a lot of laws to uphold. Beatz wasn't going to be the last person who had to suffer, per her orders. It's how everything went. Enemies had to pay.

"Lyric, letting him go or giving him the way out is breaking the commandments of the gang. As the leader, you can't break the law. And as your right hand, I can't allow you to break it," I said, plain as day. Don had to be frowning at the way she acted with pity in her heart for Beatz. Disappointed that she even wanted to show mercy to the person who took his life like that. "This is what Don would want."

"Just stop. Don't tell me what my pop would've wanted. You don't know that. Nobody knows that. I understand this is what the both of you did together, but the dead can't speak, so don't try to speak for him," Lyric snapped at me. She treated me like I had ill intentions, when all I did was follow orders and lived up to the law.

"It's a detective here to see us." Lex peeped her head in the room. I was relieved somebody interrupted, because things were about to go left quick.

"Okay. Give me a moment." Lyric looked away from Lex and back to me. "This discussion isn't over. And if this is the law of the gang then those laws are about to change." When Lyric instructed me to make Beatz pay, she was all in for him to suffer. But her conscience started getting the best of her. I wasn't sure how shit was going to work out with a wishy-washy honcho who went back on her own orders.

* * *

"You don't want this investigated?" Detective Sade frowned with her words. Lyric stepped up out of her family and looked the detective right in her face. Lyric told her they didn't want anybody on Don's case. That it was just gang-related and that they should rule it as such and to keep it moving. For them to focus on more serious cases.

Brier and Lyric bumped heads on that decision, but then she fell back and allowed Lyric to stay in control of the decisions. Everybody felt like Lyric knew what she was doing and for the most part, she did. The last thing we needed was for cops to be all up in our business. Don had a tight hold on the town and surrounding cities, but now that he was dead, we weren't sure who was still down for us or who wanted to take us down.

"No. Close the case. Drop it." Lyric upheld her decision.

"Mrs. Cotton, this is really your decision to make. Don't you want justice to be served?" Detective Sade viewed Brier with wide eyes.

"My family has gone through enough at this point and standing trial and all of that isn't worth it. This is still a tough time for us, Detective Sade. Like Lyric said, this was more than likely gang-related and running to the cops with it will only put us in more danger," Brier said.

"We can put your family under protection until the case goes to trial. And Mrs. Cotton, there's more you need to know about the surveillance foot—" Detective Sade stopped mid-sentence when Brier stood from the chair.

"Please leave," Brier said in the calmest voice.

"Okay, but if you change your minds don't hesitate to give me a call." Detective Sade gave Brier a sly smile and she excused herself from the office. A detective at HQ wasn't good for business; we had too much stuff to lose. I couldn't stop thinking about if she saw something incriminating around there or not; anything that would force her to make a trip back with more manpower. Cops were like that. They told a person what they wanted to hear, then came down on their heads and crushed them.

"Who gave her this address?" I asked out of curiosity. The men on the crew wasn't stupid enough to give any kind of law enforcement the address to HQ. It was a secret place to most, and that's how it was supposed to stay until the end of time. The way the building looked on the inside would make any person fall into question about the operations that were going on in there. It was too put together.

"I don't know." Lyric turned to view Brier and Lex, then she let herself out of the office without returning her attention to me. I felt she was still in her feelings about Beatz's condition downstairs. I couldn't let my emotions get in my way. What I was doing was a great benefit to the team.

As I was walking out of the office to check on things downstairs, my phone disturbed the task at hand. I viewed the caller ID and answered without any hesitation. I told Tara to call me if Mom Duke made any sudden turn for the worse and she was calling.

"Is everything aight?" I answered the phone with my stomach in a knot. Mom Duke was really hanging on by a thread of hair. And since that morning, Tara told me she wasn't keeping any food down and was sleeping more than before.

Tara was in tear when she laid that news on me earlier, and although I wanted to be there to help her and Oisin, I couldn't. I was in the middle of doing my part for the team while pulling Lyric's slack. Since Don's funeral, she hadn't been in the best mindset. She kept making plans, then backing out of them. She had meetings scheduled with gangs in alliance with us and missed them. Then she wasn't even looking at me the same. Whenever I was around her, she would come up with shit just to get away from me.

"I tried waking her but she won't wake up. She's breathing; she just won't wake up. I called the ambulance. I don't know what else to do, Siris." Tara broke down over the phone. Her voice was weak and all I heard was sobbing through every word.

"I'll be over in a minute," I said.

"Just be down at the hospital. I'm sure they'll make it here before you," Tara sniffled. I imagined her leaning against the wall, helpless. If I was there that day and Mom Duke wouldn't wake up, I would've lost my damn mind. To think about someone you love not waking up at your attempt to wake them was a scary thought.

"Okay." I put the phone in my pocket after the brief conversation. Usually before I left HQ, I would inform Lyric, but that day I just dipped on my own terms. She was shutting me out anyway. I figured she needed some space. I probably was sweating her too much since Don was killed. I had been there every step of the way. I saw her every day and sometimes woke next to her in the morning.

* * *

"Where is she?" I said, walking into the waiting room. I had to see

Mom Duke, hold her hand and tell her everything was going to be okay. She was a strong woman, but even a strong person needed someone in their corner rooting for them.

"She's still in the back being evaluated. The doctor will let us know when we can go back to see her." Tara embraced me without a sign of releasing me any time soon. Then she fell into a big, sad sob. Seeing her fall apart made me want to shed tears. I kept it together, though. When I cried, I cried in private. All my pain I kept bottled up inside of me with no need for it be showcased "I don't want her to go, Siris. I can't imagine life without her."

"It's gon' be aight. We gon' make it through this. We have to stay strong," I said.

"I can't be strong, I just can't. I've been gone all this time. All the lost time that I'll never get back. Out there trying to make her proud, when all along she's been sick. There was something I could've done. If I'd come home more, maybe I would've saw something was wrong and told her to get help. I just don't know." Tara continued to sob. There was no doubt in my mind that we all were going to take Mom Duke's death hard; some harder than others. I didn't have many regrets when it came down to lost time with Mom Duke. We spent a lot of time together over the years. The only thing I regretted was not making her prouder of me. Sometime during Tara sobbing on me, the doctor walked in and laid some news on us that made everything around me move in slow motion.

LEX

I know it wasn't my place and I was pissed at Beatz too, however, I couldn't allow him to be tortured like that. So, I took it upon myself to go visit the 211 Vipers, or whatever crew he repped, to somehow make them grab their balls and try to make an offer on Beatz's behalf. I never really hung around Beatz. I just knew he had to be suckered into joining a gang. I used to overhear how much he hated gang violence and all of that. Plus, hating him wasn't going to bring Michael or Pop back.

"You in the wrong hood." A tall, dark-skinned man said from behind the fence.

"Is T-Max here?" I asked.

"I am T-Max. So what's up? Ain't you Don's girl? Why are you here? Don't your folks have who they wanted?" T-Max was in no attempt to open that damn gate.

"That's why I'm here." I took a deep breath, trying to see how I was going let the words come out.

The Eastside Warriors would've been furious with me if they found out

I went to the Southside to speak with the 211s on Beatz's behalf. They were sworn enemies, but I had to do what Lyric couldn't. Although she and Beatz's were no longer friends or anything close, she still held some kind of love in her heart for him. And she was never the kind of person to fight violence with violence. "He's in pretty bad shape. Like, I'm afraid that he won't live to see another day if you don't make a phone call to my sister or Osiris. I never saw a right hand that hides in the dark when his boss was suffering at the hand of another gang. Make it right; offer them something in return of his life."

"I don't get it. He's the reason your dad is dead, and you come all the way over here to round up some help for him? What are you getting out of this?" T-Max looked past me in search of someone popping out at him with guns to raid the place.

"I'm receiving peace. I hate to see my sister go through this. For her having to murder her childhood best friend and previous lover. She loves him and I know it's taking a toll on her. I just want to get her out of the misery and free her of having that on her conscience," I said. I was the more violent one; the sister who could turn her heart cold towards a person and not look back for a second. He'd taken someone who meant the world to me besides Pop; he took my best friend. And with Mr. Griffin still angry with me and my family, I wasn't allowed to go to the funeral. I was only able to visit Michael's grave after they laid him to rest. He was my hero; the boy who took a bullet that was meant for me. He would forever be my angel looking over me. I just prayed somehow Mr. Griffin softened his heart towards me and realized I had nothing to do with Michael being shot, and that it hurt me in the worse way, too.

"How do I know this isn't a setup?" T-Max stood at the gate still looking around the place, paying close attention to his surroundings.

"Because you been in the game long enough to spot a setup. Plus, you already know the Eastside Warriors don't do setups; they just catch you slipping somewhere in public and deal with you then," I spoke half the truth. If Osiris refused to cooperate and got in Lyric's head more about

Beatz, things could've gone all wrong. It would've looked like I set T-Max up.

"Okay, fine. I'll give her a call. Lyric is in charge right?" T-Max pulled his phone out. With him agreeing to call Lyric and trying to bargain with her about Beatz, I thought, for a fact, he was going to let me inside of their HQ, but he stayed put behind the gate like a coward. "What's her number?"

"Here." I slid a white piece of paper to him through the fence and walked away. My job was done. It was up to him to either use the number, or throw it away. If he allowed Beatz to die, the blood would be on his hand, and I would go on in life knowing I did all I could.

* * *

"You taking all of this better than I would." Moomoo took a whiff of the blunt while she laid on the bed, looking up at the ceiling. Ms. Gale was gone to bible study. Moomoo told me Ms. Gale started going back to church after Pop was killed. Something about her wanting to be saved because life wasn't promised.

"How else should I take it, though? I can't mope around forever. Life still goes on; my life has to go on." I retrieved the blunt from Moomoo with tears in my eyes. I couldn't shake Michael from my mind that night. The blunt felt weak as hell that night because usually, I would be on my ass quick, but hell, I was barely feeling a buzz. "Life goes on and on."

"Lex." Moomoo raised from the bed and scooted down to where I was. She looked over and kissed me. Out of all the things she could've done, she planted a big mushy ass kiss on my lips. Out of reflex, I jumped up like a spider crawled on me. Out of the all the years she and I was cool, I never led her on in that kind of way or made her think I swung with the pussy licking gang.

"Bitch are you out of your mind? What possessed you to do some gay shit like that? Like, I ain't got nothing against a person that swings that way; I just don't fuckin' swing that way. I like dick." I wiped my lips. I didn't try to hurt her feelings; the words came out all jumbled up. For a moment, I couldn't even understand my own words through the yelling. She had me fucked up big time if she thought I was cool with some shit like that. "Why would you do that?"

"I'm sorry. I just…I thought maybe you were having the same feelings." Moomoo looked past me when she spoke those words. She looked straight ahead at the wall.

"Moomoo, you are my friend. A good friend of mine. I don't see myself with you like that. Not like that. Even if I liked girls, it would never be you," I replied, not caring how deep I hurt her feelings or how the words came out. If I even gave her an inch of that kind of feeling in return, our friendship would never be the same. Standing there in the room looking at her made it clear that it wouldn't be the same. She'd caught feelings for me and acted on them. I wasn't going to be able to look at her right. Ever. All I was going to think about was how she wanted to be with me and that bullshit of a kiss she pulled on me. She ruined the innocence of a friendship.

"I said I'm sorry, Lex. I didn't mean to upset you in no kind of way. I just thought"—Moomoo finally removed herself from the bed, and she approached me with tears in her eyes. I backed myself against the way to give us a bit of a distance—"I just thought."

"You thought wrong," I replied without sympathy of her feelings. Sympathy was something rare for me. When a person knew better, I couldn't feel a certain way for them.

"Why are you being like this?" Moomoo kept walking towards me with a look I saw in a nigga's eyes when they were persistent with their approach. I quickly moved past her, grabbed my shit off her bed and headed out. It was all wrong. The feelings she housed for me wasn't right. It was wrong. I was her friend.

When I made it outside, I almost turned right back around and went back inside. Qbaby and his homies were walking up the street towards me. He was dribbling a basketball while his boys were walking beside him talking loud as fuck. Anybody sitting out could hear their entire conversation.

"Fuck," I murmured. Going back inside meant I had to face Moomoo, see how sad she was because I turned her shot down. But staying out there meant I had to face Qbaby and explain why I didn't ever answer the phone from him. I mean, since I'd just buried my pop that was a good excuse. I could've said something about me being under the weather since the funeral. Something.

"Lex," Qbaby shouted from the road. He threw the basketball to one of his homies and ran over to me with a big ass smile on his face. "I tried to talk to you at the funeral, but you were too busy talking to everybody that popped up every ten seconds."

"Hey Q," I greeted. It was never hard for me to look at a boy, but it was hard as fuck for me to look up at Qbaby. He was standing there, taking my breath away. His chocolate skin reflected in the sun and I wanted to drown in his endless chocolate. "You should've crowd hopped like everybody else."

"Word. I'm all 'bout respecting folks though. I know how to wait my turn; wait for the right moment. Feel me?" Qbaby replied. His golds nearly blinded me from the reflection. The whole time I stood out there talking to Qbaby, I felt like somebody was staring a hole through me. I looked back only to see the drapes in Ms. Gale's living room move. Moomoo was being really crazy now, and I knew that if that's how she was going to be acting, all weird and shit, then our friendship was dead. And I wasn't going to be the bitch to revive it because I wasn't the one who messed it up. "But now that I waited my turn, when are you going to kick it with me?"

"I don't know." I finally built my nerves up to look into the eyes of that tall glass of water. I mean, really look into his eyes and connect with his soul. What I shared with Michael would forever live on; however, I had to find something to help me cope with everything. A distraction to get my mind off my hurt. Moomoo tried to be that distraction but I wasn't feeling that. The fine ass distraction I needed stood in front of me.

"Well, what are you up to now?" I asked. I hadn't ever been a scary ass girl; if I wanted to fuck with somebody that's what I did. "I mean, I don't have any kind of plans for today."

"Oh. Well, I was just going to pay hoops at the hangout with my boys. You know how that go; other crews talk 'bout how cold they are on the court, so we have to come through." Qbaby licked his lips after almost every word. Made me want to lick my own damn lips in fear that they were ashy, or even worse.

"Oh, I see." From the sound of it, he was unavailable to just kick it on such short notice. I respected it, though. Niggas on the block took basketball to heart, due to most of them having dreams about playing in college and later going to the NBA. It didn't work out for them though, so they started their own league in the hood, at the hang out my pop had built years ago.

"I can drop that, though. I can sit out if you want to hang. That game ain't that important and I'm sure there's more games like that in the future." Qbaby instantly flipped his words when he saw the disappointment wash over me. If I was a nigga, I would want to hang with me too. I was that bitch.

LYRIC

"You want to swear your alliance with us, pay off Beatz's debt, and kick him out the gang he leads? You trying to drive a high bargain. But even with all you trying to offer, it don't bring my pop back." I stood in front of T-Max with my men around us ready for whatever. He was willing to meet me down at HQ, but I didn't want him over there. There weren't many people who knew where our main location was located and I sought out to keep it that way for as long as I could. "None of the shit you offering is going to erase the past."

"No, nothing can erase the past. Nothing ever will. What he did, has already manifested. And to be honest, I take the blame for what happened. Beatz never wanted any of this. I kept putting pressure on him, trying to get him to fall into what I wanted for him. And when his life was falling apart, when he felt like he was losing you, he came to me. He was ready to give it all up, his dreams and everything, and I allowed him. Now he's in a situation he can't even get himself out of," T-Max spoke highly of Beatz. His words hit me in places I never knew words could hit. To know Beatz joined the 211 Vipers because of what was going on with Osiris and me, fucked with me in the worse way. I really didn't know what I was doing back when I started messing with

Osiris. All I remember is one minute I was rocking Beatz, then the next I was under the covers with Osiris. One thing for sure is that a person never gives up on someone they love.

"Then, if you played a part in all of this, I want you to resign from your position, too. Move far away from here. There will never be any 211 Vipers again. They will be Eastside Warriors and that's the end of it," I said, firmly. My men were giving me stares of disapproval, but I ran the show. My words were what mattered. And when Osiris finally came back after grief, he was just going to have to fall in line.

"Lyric, I...this is all I have. I can't just leave it all behind like this. The honchos who formed it worked hard to organize this gang and I worked hard to keep it together. I can't just leave it," T-Max argued. My offer was on the table. It was up to him to accept it or walk away and allow Beatz to die at my order.

"Take the offer or leave it," I said.

T-Max looked around at the men who stood around me, then he looked back at the two men who were around him. I could tell he was having all kinds of thoughts by the anxiety that crept in his eyes. Or maybe it was just bottled up fear. Possibly even anger.

"Alright. Deal." T-Max agreed to my proposition. For him to give up so much to save Beatz's life, I knew I was making the right decision by calling things even. It wasn't what Pop would've done on his enemy's behalf. I had to realize though, Pop and I wasn't the same person, and I never wanted to directly follow in his footsteps.

"Good. I'll release Beatz to you in an hour. In the meantime, you need to inform your team of the new leadership arrangements." I reached out to shake T-Max's hand then I headed out. I had a few places to be, and being there talking to him all day was making me behind on meetings. With Osiris out planning his momma's funeral, I was stuck doing everything alone. I was finally getting a deeper taste of the honcho life.

* * *

"Before you know…" Trever trailed off. Osiris told me beforehand that Trever was ready to show his face again after being caught slipping back at the warehouse. He used to be Osiris's right hand man, but they forced him to step down. I assumed Osiris was an ass to everybody walking and disbelieved in second chances, like he was higher ranked than God, himself. "He was talking 'bout getting it rebuilt. This was one of our main warehouses; the main shipment warehouse that is."

"Naw. I just want this shit torn down," I said.

"And what? You gon' buy a new one?" There was a bit of hesitation in Trever's voice. Just like Osiris, he had the audacity to side eye my decision.

"No, I'm actually in the process of closing a few and just making the others bigger." I walked around the location that was foreign to me the night of the fire. I hadn't one clue of what the fuck was going on out there.

"But Don's whole purpose of having multiple warehouses was for the company's protection. Like, if somebody raided one, we wouldn't lose the majority of the product. That's just how it's always been." Trever talked with his hands, exposing his missing finger, which brought me to a frown. I could only imagine the pain he went through when he lost his finger. Osiris told me the story one night before we went to sleep, and it made my flesh crawl all over. Made my stomach tie in knots to think about the pain that was inflicted on another person, due to an honest mistake.

"Well, he's not here anymore and last I checked, he no longer calls the shots. I run this show. There's nothing wrong with change," I spoke in confidence of my leadership. My pop had a tight hold on all the men in the gang. They did things a certain way for a long time. He forced them into loyalty by instilling fear in their hearts, but I set out to do the opposite. I wanted my men to know they were important and there was nothing to fear. I wanted them to protect me because I was good to them, not because I waved a gun around in their faces every ten minutes because I could.

"Yes ma'am," Trever said.

"And if it was up to me, you wouldn't have lost a finger or had to pay for an honest mistake. It was an honest mistake, right?" I looked over at Trever, waiting on a reply, but he didn't speak fast enough for me. When I asked a question, I needed answers right away. Then I knew for a fact, that someone was being honest with me.

"Well," Trever started. He tucked his hands in his pockets. That day was the first time the two of us were alone. Osiris was always somewhere blocking me from the whole thing. He made it seem like I couldn't function without him there. "I just let my guards down is all. It was my fault. Mistakes should never happen." For a split second, it seemed like Trever wanted to tell me something. Inform me what went down that night. Around that time, Pop kept everything a secret with Osiris covering his trails. I was still trying to figure out everything I needed to know. Osiris was still kind of keeping me in the dark on a lot of things.

"Is there something you're not telling me, Trever?" I asked.

"No. I'm sorry; I have to take this call." I never heard a phone ring and before I could ask the question for a second time, he was already across the parking complex. I wasn't one to yell out at anyone in public. I wasn't going to drop the question until it later came back to me.

In the middle of me thinking of a better way to lead the Eastside Warriors, my phone started going off and it was no one other than Osiris. Even with him out making funeral arrangements, his mind was still on the gang and what the fuck I was up to.

"Hey, handsome." I smiled as if he was standing in front of me.

"Don't give me that bullshit. Why would you make a deal with the 211 Vipers like that? Incorporate the two gangs. You just letting enemies walk into our trusted family. What's wrong with you? You love that bitch of a nigga that much you had to spare his life after everything he's done to you and your family? I don't know what to say to you right now. I'm just disappointed." Osiris flew off at the mouth with me. His anger towards me was getting old as fuck. If he wanted to be the honcho, he should've just started his own damn gang and left mine the fuck alone.

"This is my team, my people, and they abide by my rules. You're the advisor, not the fuckin' lifeline of the Eastside Warriors," I replied with the same attitude he approach me with. "Just deal with what you're dealing with. And again, I'm sorry for your loss. Goodbye, Siris."

"Is there anything you need with me before I go?" Trever slid his phone in his front pocket as he strolled across the parking lot back to me.

"Honesty keeps a man alive. Enjoy the rest of your day, Trev." I walked past him in route to the SUV. Axe was my designated driver and I didn't want him to wait too long. Plus, we had a handful of other places to stop. Back home on the Eastside was one of them. It was long overdue for me to show my face on the block and to see all the damages that were done to our property. The day Michael lost his life and Pop called me with panic in his tone as he spoke, it all happened fast and I hadn't stepped foot back out that way since.

* * *

I HOPPED out the SUV before Axe put it in park and turned off the engine. The place that I knew as home for the longest time was destroyed. All the memories, the nightmares; they were gone for good.

"Lyric." I wiped my eyes and turned around towards the driveway. Our house used to sit in the middle of the neighborhood. Before Pop built the hang out, people from all over the block used to come shoot hoops in front of our house during the summer. And, on Pop's good days, he used to go out there and join them. He tried showing me at an early age what having a true family from the same block was all about. And during those times of people shooting hoops in front of our house, I never saw any raise a gun or get tight. There were a few fights here and there, but never anything that turned completely violent. Judging by all the things that I remembered Pop doing, he had a good heart; he just managed to let his malic side triumph over it. He did good deeds, but he did worse, which brought his good to naught.

"What's up Cassie?" It was amusing to hear her even speak to me after she or her sister picked up the phone to call me to check on us. Or the fact they were really the only ones from the block who didn't show up to the funeral. Not that I was trying to pay any attention to any of that. I learned then that it wasn't the people who were for you in your prime but who stuck it out with you when you were at the end of losing everything. Out of everybody, those bitches were the ones who folded on me. Hell, there were people I wasn't cool with who were hitting up my line or messaging me on social media to check on me and my family.

"I was so worried 'bout you. And I'm so sorry 'bout Mr. Don. Such a tragedy." Cassie kept talking until she and I were standing directly in front of each other. "I'm sooo sorry."

"Yeah, are you really though? I can't even recall you hitting me up to check and see how I was doing. Not once. But you say you're my friend and shit. Used to be in my face all the damn time. Now you standing here trying to give me your deepest, fakest ass condolences. Bitch save it for someone who cares because I sure the fuck don't." I pushed past that trick and kept it moving. I was there for one reason and she wasn't that fucking reason. I left her goofy ass looking stupid as fuck. And seeing her face made me make the decision to get back focused on my music. I had bitches necks to step on. Muthafuckin' Hood Princess was to stay.

BEATZ

When I saw T-Max, all I wanted to do was fall to his knees and thank him for coming for me. For doing whatever he did to save me. My body was hurting all over, and I swear it felt like a nigga could barely breathe. The air refused to go in my lungs right.

"Get him in the truck," T-Max said. The whole time I hadn't noticed I'd fallen to the ground. My legs were too weak to stand, and I couldn't recall when the last time I even ate. "They did a number on you. You're alive though. That's all that matters."

Once we were inside of the truck, T-Max was sitting right beside me, when normally he'd be riding shotgun. Something had to be up; something serious. "211s are no more. It belongs to Lyric. I had a decision to make and I made it. All our manpower will belong to the Eastside Warriors."

"Wait? What?" It hurt to speak. It didn't stop me from summoning up a reply, though. There was no diluting all the shit T-Max went through to keep the team together throughout the years. The 211 Vipers were his lifeline; all he had in life. It's what made him look strong in the streets. He told me all the time how important it was to rep a set, and if a person didn't, the streets found a way to make a joke of them. "You serious?"

"I did it you to save you. She told me you had to step down. I had to step down, move away, and hand the remaining members over to her crew. That was the only way to save you." T-Max leaned his head against the headrest. Those words hurt me knowing the sacrifices he made for me. "I didn't want another one of Cappo's nephews to die for this gang. Enough is enough. I tried; we tried. We ruled for a while, but now it's time to give it up."

"T, I'm sorry. And if we're just being honest, I wasn't trying to murder Don that day. I really don't know how I shot him like that. Besides the training you gave me, I hadn't shot a day in my life. I thought I missed." My body was in pain that grew greater every time I spoke. It was going to be a big relief to see the doctor and recover in the safe environment of the hospital; that's if nobody decided to pay me a visit and drop me during my stay there. With the 211s no longer on the streets, there would be a target on my back even if it wasn't Lyric's decision. I just knew somebody was coming for my ass.

"You know baby savage, I've thought about that shit. Like, how sway is it for you to shoot him right above his vest. How would you know to even shoot there?" T-Max spoke those words without turning to look my way. If he believed my shots were a miss, then who the fuck killed Don that day?

"What are you saying?" When the shooting first happened, I was almost certain that I was the one to pull the trigger, but shit stopped adding up. I didn't know how to shoot.

"I'm saying, somebody staged this shit and I will get to the bottom of this," T-Max said and left it just like that. If he magically proved my innocence, then I had faith I would somehow be back in Lyric's good grace. Some fucking how.

* * *

ONE WEEK WAS behind me since T-Max made a deal to save my life, and I was on a road to recovery. The doctors released me with the strongest pain pills just three days after I was admitted. Since the 211 Vipers were shut down by the hood's princess, I couldn't stay in what used to be our HQ. My ass had no choice but to make things right between me and my momma.

"I hope you learned your lesson and know now that you don't belong out there in them streets. You're too smart to get caught up in mess like that. Too smart, Rashad." Momma parked the car next to the mailbox. She turned off the engine, staring ahead at the house. All of a sudden, I heard a sad sob coming from her. Not too long after, she broke down in a bigger sob. I was lost for words and out of ideas on how to comfort her. "I prayed so hard. I stayed up every night until late in the morning praying since you left, asking God to please watch over my child. My son."

"Momma, it's okay. I'm alright." I placed my left hand on her shoulder to soothe her. It was a sad sight to see my momma cry. To think about the pain and hurt I caused her while trying to prove a point to Lyric. Trying to look tough in her eyes, when all it did was make me an enemy to her and her family.

"No, you're not alright, Rashad. You will never be alright in this hood. In this town. Wayne stopped by here the other day. He told me what you did and how much trouble you're in because of it. You murdered Don. You're not safe." Momma finally wiped her tears. She paused for a moment before she turned to look at me. "You will take my car, use the money I give you, and get out of here. Go live with your grandma in Oregon. I can't-I can't protect you."

"I can't just run off and leave you here. It makes me a coward, and T-Max sai—" Momma cut me off by placing her finger over my lips.

"What T-Max said doesn't matter anymore. He left town days ago. You need to leave, too if you want to live out the remainder of your days." Momma placed the car keys in my hands while she viewed me with the saddest pair of eyes I ever looked into. "The money is in the glove compartment. You take it and you leave. You hear me?"

"Momma." I had just gotten my ass beat a week ago and released the same day she thought it was best for me to run for the hills.

"I'm serious, Rashad. Pack up all the shit you need to make your music and go. That's final. Use the GPS on your phone. You'll be fine. Make me proud," Momma said before letting herself out of the car.

If I was being completely honest with myself, a fresh start was what I longed for. Moving far away from Mansfield was going to give me the skills I needed. Moving to Oregon was probably going to open doors for me to move to California one day and really chase my dreams. Stack my bread up out there and hop on the dream wagon how I always intended. How Lyric and I intended. It cut me deeper thinking about it, though. Like, it was supposed to be the two of us moving out there and becoming something like Jay-Z and Beyoncé. Except I wasn't going to be doing so much rapping. All my work would be behind the scene while she was in the limelight.

"Damnit, damnit!" I punched the glove compartment so many times the skin on my knuckles were blistered. And the pain pill that I took before I left the hospital felt like it was wearing off because I felt everything from my head all the way down to my knees. Osiris made sure that I would remember his violent blows forever. He had every intention to eventually murder me. I prayed so many times during his assaults that he would get it over with and stop taking me through all the pain. I kept asking God why He just didn't take my breath. The pain was too much. I remembered the pain so well; I flinched hard as fuck when Trey knocked on the window.

"Shit." I opened the car door with my heart in my throat. "You scared me bruh."

"My bad. I just had to see it for myself. Word on the streets was that they did a number on you." Trey gave me enough space to exit the car. Back in the day, Trey and I was cool; like in middle school days. Then whenever we reached high school, he made another group of friends while I stayed isolated, working on my music. Dreaming big in the comfort of my talent.

"Well, now you see," I said. On the way to the house, I hardly recognized myself in the side mirror. I had bruises all over my face and scars I'm sure was going to stay. The small savage in me wanted to go get some revenge on Osiris and make the nigga pay for what he did. But then I realized, all my men were on his side and the Eastside Warriors' so, going up against him would be me making my own grave.

"Did you really do it? You murdered Mr. Don?" Trey was one out of a lot of people who respected Don to some point. The people who didn't agree on what he did still respected him. It's the influence he had in the hood. Don was the kind of person who talked a good game and made people forget what kind of life he led.

"Since when do you care 'bout what happens in gangs? Aren't you like the smart nigga? Should be going to college or something soon?" I tried to get Trey out of my business.

"Yeah, the plan is still in motion. But, what are you going to do with your life now? You know people got it out for you. I mean, I don't have it out for you, but people in this hood do," Trey said. His words sounded every bit like my momma's. And if they both were telling me the same thing, then I knew somebody was out there plotting my death.

"Well, that's good man. I'm proud of you. Just keep moving after college. Don't come back here." I don't know what possessed me, but I grabbed him into a brotherly embrace before we parted ways as if that was the last time I would see him. If I moved to Oregon, I was sure that was going to be our last time in each other's presence. Because once I moved, I wasn't ever planning on coming back. Not even in old age to reminisce.

Momma wanted me to go right after we made it home. Something kept telling me to wait and try to talk to Lyric one last time before I made that big of a decision. Then there was something else in me that told me to get the fuck on the road and don't look back. I was at war with myself; with my heart and conscience. They were tugging me in opposite directions.

I walked around the studio thinking back on all the time I invested in there and how much magic Lyric and I made over the years, working together being friends, then briefly lovers. She had me wrapped so tight around her finger I was willing to do anything for her. Anything. I joined some bullshit gang just to get her attention.

During the rivalry, I tried making myself believe that I no longer loved her and I could live without her. It was a lie so stupid that it couldn't stick for long. The heart longed for her. My soul ached for her touch. I wasn't going to give up on her. Not on us for a second time. Osiris had no rights being with her. She belonged to me.

I packed all my music equipment and loaded it into the car, but Oregon was going to have to see me another day because I was going to fight for my woman. It was for the better man to win. I was the man.

OSIRIS

Mom Duke had been laid to rest for almost a week. When I received that call from Tara telling me that she'd taken a sudden turn for the worse and to be at the hospital, I knew there was no coming back from that. All Mom Duke's deeds were coming to an end. Before she took her last breath, she was able to tell us what she wanted done with her body after she died. She didn't want a funeral; just a cremation and for her ashes to be dumped in the Red River. I argued with Tara for what seemed like hours because she was set on dishonoring Mom Duke's wishes. Tara was in favor of a big funeral for the entire family, then everybody come over to the house to reminisce about how good of a person Mom Duke had been to them. She wanted the whole nine yards of a funeral. Me and Oisin outnumbered her, so she backed down and fell in line like she should've done in the beginning.

While I was dealing with all the arrangements on how we were going to dump her ashes in the river, I kept getting calls about all the stupid ass decisions Lyric was making. She had the 211 Vipers under her wings. Their crew didn't even exist anymore. They were now Eastside Warriors. Our enemies were in our territory working beside us like they were part of the team since the beginning. I knew Don had to have been rolling over in his grave. Teaming up with his enemies wasn't something he ever favored. On top of all that shit, Lyric spared Beatz's life. She let the nigga walk right out of the spot, go seek medical attention and let him be. After all he did, she let him walk. It all rubbed me the wrong way and it sure as hell showed me that she still cared for him. Maybe even loved him still.

So, when Wayne called me earlier in the day, I kept Lyric in the dark. Since she was out there making decisions without me, I was going to be making a few without her. I was willing to suffer the consequences later.

"And you were serious 'bout attending this meeting alone." Wayne sat behind the mahogany desk smoking on a Cohiba Behike cigar. I didn't have to be the smartest man to know that Wayne found pleasure in showing how much money he could blow for the fun of it.

"Yeah. So, what's up?" I asked.

"The 211 Vipers already took my spot in wanting to be in partnership with the Eastside Warriors." Wayne took a drag of the cigar as he stared into a freshly poured glass of Remy Martin, the same damn whiskey that made Don a huge fan. "But I don't really want that anymore."

"Then why the fuck am I here?" It pissed me the fuck off when somebody decided to waste my time. If I wasn't there to discuss what we spoke about over the phone, there was no sense in me being in his presence. I had a whole lot of business to be catching up with than playing into his games.

"I have a friend on the force in Shreveport, a detective friend, that is. A detective that was working on Don's case before it was dropped. Like, he wasn't given a warning or anything. He just showed up and was given another assignment." Wayne inhaled a deep breath of smoke and a few seconds later, he exhaled it through his nostrils. "A case just dropped like that is a bit suspicious. Like, I don't know much about law, but I know no one can make them drop a case that's already under investigations."

"Well, a lot of people knew Don and respected him and his family. And since Brier and Lyric didn't want anyone on the case, Detective Sade dropped it. She's a detective sergeant I believe," I said.

"And that made all the sense in the world, until my friend found out the case was never dropped. They put another team on the case; a private team. And although it's private, he found some information out for me." Wayne smirked at me with the devil written all in his expression. The way he looked at me made me uneasy sitting there at the desk. I couldn't recall the last time anyone made me feel that way or managed to get under my skin. It was all new to me.

"I don't know where you're going with this." I grabbed the glass of Remy Martin he poured for me when I first arrived and took a nice gulp from it. If he kept talking to me like that, like he knew something that I didn't, I was going to need the entire bottle.

"I did some searching of my own when he laid some valuable information on me. I had one of my men to dig into something." Wayne took his own time with what he had to say. He kept me on the edge of my seat like I was front and center in a mystery film. "Timber Thibeaux's murder made ten years the day Don was killed."

"What does my brother have to do with anything?" I capped off the glass of whiskey and slammed it against the desk. I was ready to bash Wayne's head open for opening old wounds. I didn't need that kind of shit on my mind when I had just laid my Mom Duke to rest a week ago and released her ashes.

"You found out that Don was responsible for your brother's death. You got in really good with Don for like a decade, only to avenge your brother. I mean, you murdered the man who pulled the trigger. You weren't satisfied until you got the man who gave the order, which was Don." Wayne pulled his Glock ten seconds ahead of me. I removed my hand from the inside of my jacket and sat there with the world slowly slipping away from me. "I'm always one step ahead."

"What does it even matter to you?" I sat convicted. I couldn't recall a single soul being able to figure me out through the years. Don sure as hell couldn't figure me out. He thought for an entire decade that I didn't know he was the one who gave the man the order to murder my brother because he made a simple mistake like forgetting to lock up at the warehouse. Timber had been thrown out of his element the entire week leading to his death. He told me one night that he was worried and that if he died to keep his name alive out there in the streets.

"I want the Eastside Warriors to be mine for the taking." Wayne still had the Glock aimed right at my forehead. There were a few years that lied between the last man getting the ups on me. I'd never been the second man to pull out a Glock, or was the one to be beat into a corner. I learned to stay on top. The man on top won the match. It's how the game went out there.

"How am I supposed to help you with that?" I hated how things were going. Me being behind Don's death was supposed to remain in the dark until I was somewhere in my grave or his death was at least years in the past. His death was still too fresh for my name to come out like this. For the gang to know that I betrayed him. They would find a way to banish me, and unlike Beatz, I wasn't going to receive any kind of mercy. It was a fact that Lyric was going to make me suffer.

"Tell Lyric you think it's best for her to step down," Wayne said.

"She's not going to do that." I imagined leaping across the desk, pulling Wayne's tongue out his mouth and shoving up his dusty, old ass.

"She will do it or I will make sure she knows the truth. You like her, maybe even love her, right? Then I know you will make sure she does what I want her to do. And you can still serve as the right hand for the Eastside Warriors, I mean the Serge Gs, since we'll be one big team."

Wayne placed the Glock on the desk. With him having his guards down, I could've placed a bullet through his dome. But I couldn't. If he knew about my truth, then I was sure it was a handful of other people who knew and would go rat me out the moment I dropped Wayne. I had to play the shit smart if I wanted to survive long enough to hash out a plan.

"You have a deal." I headed over to the door. I bit down on my teeth so hard, it felt like they were going to shatter in my mouth.

"I knew you would come around." Wayne walked behind me to the door. It took everything inside of me not to just blast him away and think about a plan later. However, I walked my ass out that office with my tail tucked and kept it moving.

* * *

"Is this your way of apologizing for acting like a dick to me lately?" Lyric walked into the hotel room in the sexiest red dress I ever saw a woman in. Her curves were exposed like roses in the peak of spring. And the confidence she wore made me want to get down on one knee and seal the deal. If I was smart, that's what I would've done right away without anyone knowing except the two of us. Then whatever she owned would belong to me, too.

"Yeah, you can say that. I know I haven't been the best boyfriend to you." I led her into the bedroom while holding her left hand. Everything about the moment felt right. It wasn't though; it was all wrong. If anybody was innocent in the whole thing, it was Lyric. She had nothing to do with the hatred I had towards Don. And I didn't try to drag her into it. I wasn't able to help myself, though. Since she turned the legal age of consent, I'd been wanting to fuck with her.

"Oh, so you're my boyfriend?" Lyric said. I stopped in my tracks, turning to look at her. She was clearly testing me. She was my girl and she put that shit in question like that. Almost broke my savage of a heart.

"What? You seeing another nigga?" I said.

"If I were, you wouldn't even be in here right now." Lyric moved past me. The whole night we were together, she was a bit distant than she were before. She kept giving me smart-ass replies and short conversation. She barely tried to keep me entertained over dinner at the fanciest restaurant in the city. After she made a few of her own decisions out there, I figured she would be in the best mood a person could be in.

"Aye, what's your fuckin' problem? You holding back something I don't fuckin' know? Is there a problem with us that I need to address?" I got tight on her ass for a second. I was professional about all my approaches; she was testing me though. Pushing all my damn buttons. I never had to run a bitch down for nothing.

"Nigga what? Are you even serious right now? Don't be coming at me like that yo, you be fuckin' bugging," Lyric snapped back at me. Instead of staying on that level with her, I walked over to her, wrapped my hand around her throat, and shoved her into the wall while I ripped her underwear off. The whole time she allowed me to take charge of her. I had been living long enough to know all women wanted to be dominated; even the bitches who think they are alphas. Dick them down one good time while being in control, and they were going to be hooked for a lifetime.

"Now what were you saying?" I asked while I slid into her tight pussy. Her pussy was tighter than any pussy I'd had in a long ass time. She never was around the block like most girls. She had that grabber that was able to suck a man in and hold him until after they both fell into ecstasy.

"I said-I said—I fuckin' love you, Siris. I act crazy and all that shit, but somehow during all of this, I fell hardddd." Lyric talked to me in the sexiest tone. Her words shocked my soul. I was no Saint; nothing close to the man she thought I was. I was an enemy in her midst. A man who knew how to disguise himself as a nobleman.

"I love ya ass too, girl," I said through the best feeling I ever felt.

Lyric, she was just the kind of woman that took a man by surprise. She stood her ground and didn't waiver from what she believed was right. I respected that about her, no matter how much I hated it in the same sense.

"Ouuu, it feels so good. You make me feel so good." Lyric draped her arms over my shoulders as she took all of me. I removed her from the wall and carried her over to the bed. We weren't fucking; we were making intense love while being crazy in love. I refused to let the worry tug at me, because I knew if I did what Wayne asked of me, she and I could move the fuck away and start our lives over. Be together without anyone trying to get between us. I was thinking about moving far away, possibly out of the states. I couldn't risk someone breaking up what we shared. I just couldn't.

I laid her on the bed, made her scoot to the edge. She placed her legs in the air and I made sure they were on my shoulders. I wanted her to take all of me. To take every inch like she wanted it to touch her fucking soul. I was certain I was giving her all the things the other nigga who shared a piece of her heart never gave her. He was a young nigga, and a young nigga was never able to compete with a fully-grown man who was experienced in all departments.

"Ouuuuu, my fuckin' godddd. Oh my god, Siris. Fuck. I feel you in my stomach. Ohhhh babe." Lyric was hitting all kinds of notes with her screams. She was so in sync with her moans, it sounded like a whole damn song in there. She was screaming so loud, I knew we were disturbing the people beside and below us in the hotel, but I didn't care. I was too focused on trying to snatch her fucking soul.

"Yeah, take this big dick." I pounded into her harder than before, trying to knock her fucking walls loose. She needed to understand I wasn't the kind of man she could play with; get smart with whenever she wanted to. I aimed to show her just how bad it could get. It went from lovemaking to me intentionally trying to hurt her. Hurting her wasn't part of my plan for the night. I just somehow got too carried away.

"You love having a fuckin' attitude with me. You better fuckin' learn who the fuck you talking to like that. You understand me, bitch?"

"Ouuch, wait. That hurts. Babe, it hurts. Go slower. I can't take it," Lyric begged through a few moans for me to take it easy on her. I refused to listen. I was too damn persistent to stop. Plus, my mind never worked that way, I couldn't stop when I was determined to prove a point. She had to pay.

"Take this dick." I thrust deeper and deeper until my body locked up for a second and I busted all inside her pussy without allowing her to climax.

LEX

Pop being gone gave me all kinds of freedom; like the freedom of waking up in bed with a boy after having a wild ass time. Qbaby was exactly the distraction I needed. If it was temporary, it was okay with me. I couldn't see myself with him for a long ass time. I was young and he; well he was older and could have just about anybody. I was more than sure young and old hoes flocked to him.

"You slept good, lil' shawty?" Qbaby hopped out the bed butt ass naked and his dick was still hard. His morning wood was knocking, and my inexperienced ass wouldn't take all that for a third time in under twenty-four hours.

"Yeah, I slept great." I sat up in bed with the covers pulled up to my chest. As much as I wanted to feel bad for getting underneath another boy when Michael's death was still so damn fresh, I fought the feeling away. I had to learn how to move on by sweeping my feelings under the rug and not looking back on the past and all the damn what-ifs.

"That was your first time being with a nigga in that way." It sounded like Qbaby was asking a question. It was a statement though. He found out the truth after I kept screaming when he tried just sticking his dick in me like I had slept with the whole block. Michael and I did some things, like oral sex and dry humping, but never the real deal. We both were waiting until we built our nerves up. Like, let it would just happen without putting pressure on each other. It never happened though; he was taken too damn soon from me.

"I mean, I wasn't given all the freedom like those other bitches. My pop stayed in my business. Always made sure I was hanging 'round the right crowd. He used to sweat the hell out me yo." It was crazy admitting my relief to some nigga who was really just a stranger in passing, until about a week ago. When Pop was alive, Qbaby made sure he kept his head the other way and never tried to get all up in my face like that. I mean, he spoke sometimes; that was it though. Everybody used to speak. Now there were niggas coming out of the bushes trying to holla.

"That's a good thing. Don't let these hoes fool ya. They be wishing they had a dad to look out for them out here. Niggas are savage as fuck out here. Do a bitch stray dog bad." Qbaby walked into the bathroom that was connected to his bedroom. At only nineteen, the nigga had his own spot. He told me that his momma was on crack and his dad was absent, so he fended for himself and hustled until he was comfortable. I gave him props; he was doing something most young niggas complained about not being able to do. He was funding his damn self.

His words made my throat go dry. I felt like balling up underneath the covers and never showing my face again. He made it seem like I took my old life for granted. And it was the truth. I was too busy complaining about all the things that I had to sneak to do, not realizing how many girls would kill to be in my shoes, regardless of all the pain I was going through behind closed doors.

"You straight." Qbaby woke me out of my dark thoughts.

I smiled up at him. "I'm fine. I'm good. I better get going, though."

"Did I do some wrong?" Qbaby must've noticed the smug look on my face or peeped that I was over thinking about something.

"No. I just have to get going. I don't want to overstay my welcome." I hopped out the bed with the cover wrapped around me. My clothes were on the dresser. I left them there before we got freaky the night before. I felt dirty though. I hadn't ever woken up and changed into the same dirty clothes from the day before. And it wasn't like I was able to go up the street and put on some clothes because our house was burned to ashes, blowing in the wind and shit.

"You can put on some of my gym shorts and a shirt if you wanted to freshen up before you leave." Qbaby was being sweet as fuck to me. Like, I knew sex was his number one priority, however, he tried not to make it obvious.

"Thank you, because I didn't want to drive that far without having a bath and changing clothes." I shot him an appreciative smile.

"You're welcome, lil' shawty. You mind if I hop in with ya, though? I need a shower too. A shower and you know." Qbaby showed his shiny ass grills. He took my soul when he did that. It was like he could flash his grill and it instantly made me intoxicated.

"Then come on," I murmured.

* * *

"So, this what you doing now? Ignoring me and being under random niggas?" Moomoo came at me all sideways in route to the SUV. Last I checked, Qbaby was the only nigga I had been messing around with or even giving the time of day to. She had me fucked up if she thought I was going to allow her to drag me like that.

"Random niggas? Bitch are you smoking lightbulbs? You have some fuckin' nerves to come at me like that. And what I do is my fuckin' business." I continued my route to the SUV. My pussy was in pain from the wild ass time I had with Qbaby and I didn't need to be out there fighting that hoe ass bitch in that kind of position.

"Why you keep trying to fight who you truly are? You know you feeling me, so why you not acting like it? You afraid of what people will think about you? 'Bout us?" Moomoo was damn near yelling our business across the street, down the street, or wherever people were able to hear her loud ass. I just didn't want Qbaby to come out the damn house to listen to all the shit she was saying. She sounded crazy as fuck out there, making a fool of herself in public.

The last time I spoke to Moomoo was the day she decided to make a pass at me; a pass that I turned the fuck down with the quickness. I told her I didn't swing that way and I left her to deal with whatever feelings she had for me. I wasn't going to be part of that bullshit. If she wanted a girlfriend, then there were a lot of girls that swung that way and would've loved the hell out her at some point.

"Bitch what are you talking 'bout? Don't you know that if I really was that way I would be open 'bout that shit? There's no shame in my game. I'm just not digging you like that or any other girl for that matter. I want to be your friend, that's it. Be tight like we used to be as fuckin' friends." I stopped in my tracks when I peeped the bitch hadn't stopped walking behind me. I knew enough to know not to turn my back for long on a person who was pissed because they were capable of doing anything.

"Why are you doing this, Lex? Why?" Moomoo broke down in front of me. A part me felt bad while the other part didn't give a damn about any waterworks.

"Moomoo, just stop. You making yourself look desperate as fuck. You a beautiful girl, built like a stick but beautiful. Somebody will be happy to be with you. That somebody is just not me." I broke it to her in the simplest way. Then I took quick strides towards the truck and didn't slow down until I was inside and she was standing in the driveway looking like a damn fool.

After that part of the day was behind me, I made my way to the new three-bedroom townhouse in Shreveport that was now our home. Momma was still openly dealing with her grief of losing Pop, but she made sure she took care of business and her girls. Well, two of her girls, because Lyric was out there taking care of herself. I hadn't seen her since she told that detective to basically kick rocks.

Boni was sitting in the living room watching Little Women, the nineteen ninety-four version, which was the best version if it was ever in question. Whenever I wasn't out getting away from home, I used to hip her to all the older movies. It was how we used to bond. But, the last few weeks that was behind us put a strain on our bonding. I was too busy trying to deal with my grief than to check in on my little sister. The youngest of us.

"I see you hooked on this movie." I flopped on the couch beside Boni. At twelve, she was aged beyond her years. She was standoffish from a lot of people, however, when she opened her mouth to really have a conversation, her smartness showed. And when someone pissed her off, and she built her nerves up, that flip ass mouth showed too, and made it really clear who her older sisters were.

"There's nothing else to watch on TV," Boni said in the driest tone I ever heard her have with me. Made me feel like I was cramping her space or something.

"Yeah, it be like that sometimes. Have you tried getting out of the house?" I looked over at Boni. She stood up from the seat and placed her hands on her hips like she was about to serve me with the smartest reply that could ever be spoken to another person.

"How the hell am I supposed to get out the house when Momma is too busy searching for jobs like she need one? Lyric isn't anywhere to be found and you, I don't know where you be now." Boni gave me all kinds of attitude. I refused to hold her to it though; she was going through the wringer like the rest of us. She had to deal with hers alone while the rest of us was out finding ways to get our minds off it.

"Then I apologize. I can take you somewhere today. Where you wanna go?" I asked.

"To my fuckin' room." Boni rolled her eyes and walked out the living room. I set my mind on going after her, then decided against it. She was going to come around when the time was right for her. There was no good in me following behind her trying to make her do what I thought was best.

LYRIC

I went to sleep with a man I didn't even know. I'd spent so much time with him since before Pop was murdered, I felt like I knew him. I fell in love with Osiris despite my first intuition. Something deep inside of me told me to steer clear of him. The other part of me forced me to see what was behind him and his persona.

"I think you should step down Lyric. I've been doing some thinking. Like, you should let all of this go and chase your dreams. I will go with you. My Mom Duke is dead, Don is dead, and I don't want to lose anyone else if I can help it." Osiris came out of nowhere with those words.

"So, since I'm making decisions out here, you in your feelings and want me to back down? I thought you were born to ride for the gang. You were supposed to be my right hand." I removed myself from the bed. I no longer wanted to be beside him.

"Lyric, this ain't the life for you. Look how you let an enemy go on your watch. Don't you know you can't trust an enemy to let shit like that go? Tomorrow you can walk out the house and catch a bullet in your dome. That's how shit is out here. Niggas catch you slipping and that's the end of you; end of your life." Osiris kept crowding my space. When we made it to the hotel, I wasn't in the mood to even be with him in any kind of way. I almost canceled the dinner. Things were rubbing me the wrong way about him. He had a secret meeting with Wayne and I was in the dark on what they discussed. For all I knew they were plotting against me.

"You go have a meeting with Wayne without telling me? Is that what we do now? Tell me, since you know so much about the gang, about what Pop would want. All his likes and dislikes. Tell me, what the fuck kind of punishment would he give his right hand for doing some shit like that?" I slid my dress back on.

Back when Osiris was out and Trever was filling in, he told me things that made me remove the trust I had in my heart for Osiris. Told me things like Pop was the one who gave the order to the man who murdered Osiris' brother. And that Osiris knew all that information for years. But part of Trever's word didn't sit well with me. If Pop knew Osiris was aware of the truth, he would've never trusted him as any kind of high-ranked member of the Eastside Warriors. I made a split-second decision, dropped Trever in the truck and had Axe to clean up the mess, then I dropped his ass too and left him out there to rot on side of the road.

"Lyric you made stupid decisions. I couldn't risk you trying to do business with Wayne. I couldn't." Osiris made it seem like he was only looking out for my best interest, when all he was doing was trying to cover up shit he'd done. "I just met with Wayne and told him straight up that we ain't doing any kind of business with him. That's what he wanted. You know that."

"How long you knew Pop was behind your brother's death?" I stood next to the dresser with my heart racing. I knew shit could've went left real quick, but I was willing to take that risk to see what he had to say and if it added up. "How long Mr. right hand?"

"Lyric what are you talking 'bout?" Osiris finally started to approach me. He had a Glock stashed in the dresser drawer and another was in his overnight bag. While he was sleeping soundly, I took the clips out and tossed them in the trash. I had a Glock loaded in my purse that was right beside me, resting on the dresser. When Trever told me what was up and how Osiris was coming, I was in tears all day, knowing a person I loved, did me completely in. The way he had me thinking he was for me, when he was just in it to get this own revenge, troubled my soul. It made me vomit in my mouth a few times thinking how I laid down with him and let him have his way, only to find out he was against me all along.

"How long did you know?" I grabbed my Glock out my purse before he made any farther steps. He had me for the wrong one if he thought that after finding out what I found out he was going to walk free without a care in the world.

"Lyric." Osiris placed his hands in the air. His eyes went straight to the dresser, then they fell to his pants.

"Don't even think about it. Your guns are empty, Trever is dead and so is Axe. Now tell me the damn truth." Tears leaped out my eyes, as my finger grew tighter around the trigger. My anger was different towards Osiris than Beatz. After all the shit Beatz did or was supposed to be responsible for, I found pity in my heart for him. While I stood there in front of Osiris, all I wanted to do was pull the trigger and get it over with.

"Lyric, you and I was never supposed to happen. Not this deep. I was putting up an act for so long; so long. So, when Don told me he wanted me to be with you, I took him up on that offer because hell, in a way, I was feeling you anyway. I got so caught up, I took my eyes away from the real goal." Osiris took a step forward. My hands were trembling around the gun and my headache was on one hundred. I pulled the trigger and he was already heading inside the other part of the hotel room. I kept firing shots through the wall until I thought he was hit. He had to pay for being an enemy in disguise. He was right beside Pop for all those years at a time, then he preyed on me as a foolish target.

Osiris had a strong pull within the Eastside Warriors, so I wasn't sure who was on his side or against him. I couldn't call anyone. I had to fend for myself. And after everything was said and done, I was going to be able to weed out the fake from the real. Starting by keeping the men who had been on the team the longest and banishing the niggas who were new recruits.

"Get that bitch," I heard Osiris yell out an order. When we fell asleep after coming there following dinner, I knew for a fact that there wasn't anyone else in the room, or not even a guard following us for that matter. We were alone, or at least that's what I thought.

I cocked the Glock back, and repositioned my finger around the trigger, ready for whoever was about to come inside of the room to get me, per Osiris' request. When I saw somebody come at me, I fired a shot and missed, tried to cock the Glock back again but I was too slow. When I looked up Gates already had his arms wrapped around me and was carrying me out the hotel room. I kicked, screamed, and cursed. I was doing everything to get some attention from the other guests who staying inside of the hotel. With all the gunshots, I was sure somebody had called the cops, but I was in desperate need for somebody to intervene. In the middle of me trying to fight for my life, I felt a heavy bang against my head and everything around me started to spin like I was on a merry-go-round.

"Damn did you kill her?" I heard Gate's voice right before everything went black.

* * *

OSIRIS WAS LOOKING RIGHT at me while he sat in a black, tore up leather chair. He had a blunt in one hand and a Glock in the other. The room was dark, and we were the only two inside. I wasn't going to be surprised if he pulled the trigger on me, because if the tables were turned, I sure as hell was going to send him away.

"Wakey, wakey, wakey." Osiris blew smoke haloes. Judging from his posture, he was calm sitting there in front of me while I was restrained to a chair. "You not very smart. You know that right?"

"Where you think you're going to go after you kill me?" My lips felt swollen, busted up.

"I'm gon' live the same life I've always led. You have to know one thing, after the main honcho dies, so does the loyalty people housed for him. The team is going to side with me because you know most of them didn't agree with what you did with letting members of the 211s join." Osiris took a drag of the blunt, holding the smoke in for a long second before exhaling through his mouth. The smoke was thick, like a cloud caused by a tornado. "I might let your lil' family live or maybe I'll off they ass too."

"Why? What are you getting out of this? You have me and you let me fall in love with you knowing your intentions were ill. I put my trust in you. Had me believing you cared 'bout us, about me, but I was just some pussy to fuck while you figured out what you were going to do." Tears were so thick in my eyes, I was barely able to see anything ahead of me. His face was just a blurred image to me until the tears finally released from my eyes and traveled down my cheeks like a waterslide.

"You weren't supposed to find out. To be honest, I was feeling you too, Lyric. I fell in love with your spunk, and all that damn sass you have. You took me by surprise, too. You did. But then you showed me your true colors. You're a weak lil' girl who let her heart get in the way of business. That's what makes me different from a lot of people; I can love someone and still complete the task at hand." Osiris rose from the chair; made it look like he just floated to his feet he was so smooth.

"Why would you do this? If you wanted Pop dead, why you just didn't kill him before attaching yourself to his crew and to his fuckin' life? You really had revenge in your heart for ten whole years, Siris. You been plotting for ten years. What really happened that day? Did Beatz shoot him or did you?" I knew my face had to be a mess. Snot and tears were falling like rain during a thunderstorm.

"Sometimes a good plan takes a long ass time. I must admit too, Don kind of grew on me over the years. I started to really look up to him, until I had to wake my damn self up and focus on the task. Separate feelings from business. It's simple. And to be honest, that day you decided to invite Beatz to the hotel, I just wanted to get it over with. So, I called Don up and told him the nigga was on his way. Don was already aware that Beatz had made a few minor hits at him." Osiris stood over me like the monster he was. His eyes were barely visible in the dimmed lighting, but I imagined them dark and filled with a violent kind of evil. "Beatz did shoot him that day, but not to kill him. See, Don was wearing a vest. He always wore a vest on the streets. He fell because he tripped over something on the ground, and I told Axe to take you inside. That's when I fired the shot right in his neck. See, that lil' square nigga couldn't pull some shit off like that. I murdered the muthafuckin' honcho."

BEATZ

"You didn't do it. You know his own right hand was the one who pulled the trigger?" T-Max spoke over the phone after supposedly skipping town due to a deal he made with Lyric to save me from her wrath. T-Max came through for me once again. Although, at the time I boasted about killing Don, a part of me was disappointed in myself for falling into that kind of trap. Don was Lyric's dad and if I cared for her in the way I claimed, I would've never joined a gang to plot her dad's downfall. It was clear that I didn't pull the trigger, but all the dirt I did felt like the blood was still on my hands.

"Osiris?" My head spun with the information. If Osiris pulled the trigger, there was no doubt in my mind that Lyric was in trouble. If he pulled the trigger, he had a bigger plot than anybody could imagine.

"Yeah. You know his brother used to be part of the Eastside Warriors. Don had the nigga banished due to him dropping the ball on something dealing with business. Osiris murdered the man responsible, but he still had one person on his list." T-Max finally laid the rest of the information on me.

I was still in town after Momma told me to get my ass out of sight and out of mind. The car was loaded with my belongings, the tank was full, and it was easy to hop on the highway and go ghost. But I refused to leave Lyric in the arms of somebody who didn't mean her any good.

"Thank you man. Although you're the reason I was in that bullshit, I thank you for watching out for me. I'm 'bout to call Lyric now to inform her." I sat in the car frozen behind the steering wheel for a moment.

"Be careful." T-Max dropped the call.

I was still shook. The short time I was around T-Max he put me on game, but he never told me that somebody so close to you could be your worse enemy. My mind went straight to the shit I did toward Lyric. I was close to her but managed to fuck shit up for her. Hadn't I burned down the warehouse with T-Max and gave Ruffis and the other dude orders to scare Lex, none of it would be happening. As I sat in the car deep in my thoughts, all the shit was starting to add up. The day I was at the hang out trying to stir up my own pot for Don, Osiris had already made his attempt of burning down their house. Because I swore to my last breath that trying to burn Brier and Boni up in a house fire wasn't part of my plans.

I dialed Lyric with my heart beating too damn loud. So loud I was barely able to hear the damn phone ringing in my ear. "Lyric?"

"Oh, y'all back friends now? See this is why I know you ain't a good fit for the team." I heard Osiris over the phone. His words were hostile towards Lyric.

"Help!" I heard Lyric scream from the top of her lungs. I heard a noise jump at me through the phone and everything fell silent. I didn't know what to think. My brain tried coming up with the worst-case scenario; I managed to push it all aside though because I didn't want to think he was harming Lyric in any kind of way.

"What you want with Lyric? Punk ass nigga?" Osiris spoke over the phone. He sounded out of breath like he'd been running.

"It's none of your fuckin' business what I want with Lyric. Just let me speak with her." I wanted him to hear no kind of fear in my voice, so I kept my tone firm, matching the masculinity.

"Oh, you think you have heart now because you pulled the trigger on Don and Lyric let your lil' clown ass walk? You think you tough out here in these streets' nigga? Well, let me tell you, I don't do a whole lot of talking," Osiris said.

"You pulled the trigger on Don. Did you tell Lyric that?" Those words flew out of my mouth at the wrong damn time. I wasn't supposed to tell him that I knew. Those words, the truth, was for Lyric to hear not the monster who was playing both sides of the game.

"She already knows and that's why she's suffering at my hand now. You lil' kids don't know how to play the game, deal the hand. You start acting different then speak on a man's truth like that's supposed to put fear in his heart," Osiris spoke at me through what sounded like a chuckle. My right hand tightened around the steering wheel as if I had the strength to bend it.

"You better not hurt her," I said.

"Did you hear anything I said? Nigga, she's suffering at my hand. She's fucked. Now what are you going to fuckin' do?" Osiris ended the call with his final word and left my head hurting in fear of Lyric's life. With his truth out in the open, there was no telling what he was planning on doing to her.

"Damnit, damnit, damnit." I started the engine and pulled out of the driveway, finally, after sitting in the car for almost an hour, and called Lex a few times with no luck. All I knew was that they were living in Shreveport, so I was in route up there hoping I wasn't making a blank trip. Aside from trying to reach Lex, I sent her a few texts informing her what kind of trouble Lyric was in and that it was Osiris who pulled the trigger on Don. I was driving so fast down the Holly road to get to the main highway, I knew for a fact my messages read like a bunch of gibberish.

***

"I TRIED CALLING HER TOO; no fuckin' luck." Lex paced around the parking lot with her hands on top of her head. She agreed to meet with me after I kept burning her phone up about Lyric. The whole time we were out there, Lex was beating herself up for not seeing through Osiris's bullshit before Lyric's life was hanging in the balance. "I hope he didn't do anything stupid. I alerted a few of the Warriors on her behalf, Gates being one of them. He, of all people, wasn't fond of Osiris after he was forced to step down from his position."

"What are they going to do?" I sat on the hood of the car out of plans and leads. I tried calling Lyric's phone again in hopes that I would get an answer to buy her more time.

"Gates is organizing a search party." Lex finally stopped walking around and I was thankful because watching her walk around like that was making me dizzy.

"You sho he's to be trusted? And you don't know where Lyric and Osiris could be? Do you have her Apple ID? Anything like that that can give us her exact or an old location in the last twenty-four hours." I slid off the hood and grabbed my phone off the charger in the car.

"Lyric is a very secretive person when it comes down to passwords, Apple IDs and shit. She lives for people to not know her business." Lex got in on the passenger's side and sat in the seat. With the two of us in deep thought, I had no doubt that an idea was going to present itself to one of us.

"I feel so stupid for thinking she deserved a person that like that. I should've fought harder instead of stooping to his level. I got caught up and my anger got the best of me. I just wanted to show her that I was able to be a hood nigga if that's what she wanted, but I went 'bout it the wrong way." I spilled half of my heart out to Lex. If I spilled the other half, I probably would've been in tears in front of her, making myself look like a big ass sissy.

"You breaking down right now isn't going to help the situation. You made a mistake, I fuckin' get it, but now Lyric is in trouble. In big ass trouble. I think we should get the cops involved." Lex moved her thumbs over her phone quicker than my eyes could blink.

"Won't she get in trouble with the cops being involved since she played a hand in the gang? What if he tells them his side of the story; tell them 'bout all the things she was involved with? What happens to her?" I was focused on the bigger picture. Trying to make sure Lyric got a clean slate was my primary focus. Don was killed and Lyric stepped up to the throne to live out his duties. She put her life on hold for a short while to walk in her dad's shoes. It was tragic to watch. The kind of tragic that gripped a person's heart and slung them across the highway to be run over.

"We can't think about that. I just want her safe and we'll deal with whatever consequences comes after all of this. If she lives, she lives to get back on her path, but if she dies, Osiris wins. He truly wins." Lex input a number in her phone, her mind was made up on what she was going to do.

"It's 'bout time you answered the phone. You have a serious choice to make, Siris. You can let Lyric go, walk away and never show your face back up in town, or you can answer to the cops because trust me, I have Detective Sade on speed dial. All I have to do is let her know that the killer is 'bout to strike again," Lex said, putting the phone on speaker so I was able to hear Osiris's reply and to record his every damn word. We were playing it smart now.

BANG! BANG! BANG!

"Go to the fuckin' cops if you want to and your sister will be dead. I don't do fuckin' threats lil' bitch." Osiris breathed into the phone, heavily. The gunshots forced my eyes closed. Just knowing he had the upper hand and could kill Lyric if he wanted, made my anger spring into overdrive.

"You kill her and I will kill you. But I gave you a choice." Lex hung up the call without checking to see if Lyric was okay or not. That's all I wanted to know. Like, was she breathing?

"We have to get the cops involved. We have too." Lex shook her head, looking ahead at the gas station.

"You heard him. He will kill her if we get the cops involved," I replied, still focused on Lyric walking away from him alive.

"Beatz, he's going to kill her even if the cops don't get involved. You think a man like that is going to let her walk willingly? We just have to hit him with all we can. At least getting the cops involved will help us get a location somehow," Lex spoke, certain of her decision while I was still looking at all the cons of her plan.

"Figure out her fuckin' Apple ID password and email address so I can use Find my iPhone. Then, we can pull up and sneak him. We can work together as a team," I said.

"Do you even know how to shoot?" Lex turned around to look at me. For a second, we both were quiet and then broke down in laughter. We laughed until the moment turned back into reality and she shed tears. Shit was crazy. I mean, over the top crazy. None of our plans seemed good enough; not good enough to get Lyric back in one peace. Lex couldn't bargain with him with money because he was already loaded in cash. We changed our plans six times in under an hour. We weren't going to give up, though. Lyric was coming home, unharmed.

OSIRIS

"Lex called me. She wanted me to do a search for Lyric." Gates stood in the hallway next to the door. If Lyric and her family really was involved with the gang, they would've known all the locations off the back of their hands and it would've been easy for them to find me. But since Don kept them in the dark about a lot of things over the years, he set them up for their downfall.

"Well, you better get that search party going man," I said through a light chuckle while lighting a blunt for the third time in one damn day. I hadn't smoked that much since my brother was killed and I stayed up hour upon the hour trying to figure out what the fuck I was going to do to avenge him. My nerves were shot. My truth was out there in the streets for everybody to know and I didn't like that one bit. Wayne and I had a deal; a deal that was off the table now since Trever ran his bitch ass mouth to Lyric and probably the whole damn town.

"Man, you the boss," Gates spoke highly of me. Over the years of working with Don, Gates and I couldn't stand to be in each other's company, but right at the end of my plan, I found favor in his eyes, and he in mine. We were working together as a team. He had it in for Don for snatching his position from him and I had my own damn reason to hate the nigga. Don was vicious and selfish. It was all about him and his fucking entitled family. I gave him props; he worked for all the things he owned and the gang he ran, but just like all the other niggas in power, he let it get to his head and thought he could do whatever he pleased. And for years, that's exactly what he did. He shitted on any and everybody who went against him.

"Naw, I'm no boss. I'm just smart when it comes down to this street shit. Can't trust anybody." The weed was hitting in ways it hadn't the first two times during the day.

"Shid, you killed the boss. I don't know if you know, but that makes you one hell of a nigga out here. Don was a hard man to overthrow, due to the kind of pull and respect he has out there on the streets. You did some ruthless shit bruh." Gates kept speaking highly of me. Too damn high. I saw right through his damn act. He helped me all the way down to the last damn minute, until he fucking folded.

"What did you do?" I grabbed the Glock from my waistband and aimed a clean shot at his head. Don trained his entire crew to aim between the eyes. Niggas survived gunshots to the legs, arms and stomach sometimes, but he couldn't recall a man walking away after being shot in the head. The dome was the primary target. "What did you do bruh?"

"Man where the fuck is this coming from? I thought we were on the same team, fighting for the same damn reason." Gates looked up and saw death hovering him. I decided against allowing him to see another day. What he did for me was a good deed in my eyes and I was grateful for the strings he pulled and all that. However, all good things must come to end someday, and not all friendships are meant to last forever.

"We were fighting for the same team, but you think I don't see the way you look at Lyric every time she's in your presence? I don't know why or when you started feeling that way towards her, but I know a man that has feelings for a woman isn't to be trusted when the plot is against that woman." I fired a shot, placing a hole right above his heart.

Popping a nigga in the dome was Don's style, but I found joy in making them suffer. To allow them to feel the pain; all of the pain. I enjoyed telling them their transgressions before they met the Maker or whoever niggas met afterlife. "But you turned into a rat, right? You told that bitch where we are."

"Si, man please." Gates held the gunshot wound distorted, in disbelief that he'd been found out so soon. I kept telling niggas though, that I was a fucking monster out there. I was smart when it came down to the streets. I lived for the streets for so damn long, that's all I knew.

"Please?" I questioned. The sight of the bright-red blood made my soul happy. My brother was fully avenged and I was just tying up loose ends. And if the cops didn't have any concrete evidence that I was the one who pulled the trigger, I was going to be walking out a free man on a mission to start my own damn team with niggas I knew were riding for me. "Nigga you supposed to go out like a soldier, not some punk ass bitch."

PHEW! PHEW!

I let my suppressed Glock rip that nigga's chest out some more. His chest went up and fell right back down. He was a fucking goner. He died at my hand, like all the other niggas who tried to cross me throughout the years. I wasn't one to be messed with in the slightest way.

*　*　*

"Why are you doing this? I thought we had something special, Siris?" Lyric kept trying to play mind games with me. I was nowhere near falling into her damn trap, though. "I thought you loved me. That you were going to be my protector."

"Lyric, you fucked that up when you decided to empty all my clips while you thought I was sound asleep and when you decided to fuckin' question me like I'm a damn child. Then you had the nerves to pull a gun on me. I think we both know the love ran out the door when you shot at me." I took my seat in front of her again. I was in the middle of figuring out what the hell I wanted to do with her; how I wanted to kill her for crossing me.

"Can you blame me though? You sat in my face and lied to me. You fed me all I wanted to hear only to bite me in the back. Then that night you treated me like a bitch out on the streets selling her body for a few dollars," Lyric fussed. I took it easy on her, slapped her around once when she first woke up after getting hit across the head for screaming in the hotel. She was bringing too much damn attention to us. Gates was being too damn gentle with her, allowing her to kick and scream like a child. I didn't do noise. That was a lesson she had to learn quickly.

"Lyric, you know this can only go one way now. I can't allow you to walk out alive. That's not even lawful to me. Allowing my enemy to lurk amongst me only to later plot for my downfall. We're already too damn far gone." I said those words and left her in the room. I had a meeting with Wayne. He still wanted the Eastside Warriors for the taking, even when I took the deal off the table. And all of a sudden, I was set on handing them to him. I had a bigger, more thought-out plan for myself. I refused to stand beside him as any kind of right hand; my days of answering to another man had come to an end. No more sitting in the hot chair praying I didn't upset the boss or brought shame to the team, due to my actions. None of that. Instead, I was going to be the one in charge, making niggas afraid to cross me. With Wayne taking the Eastside Warriors and initiating them into his crew, he was going to have the biggest team in the state. At least until my team hit the ground running, ready to take over territories.

Since I couldn't trust anyone else around Lyric, I asked Jab to just be in the building to make sure nobody got inside to try and save her. He agreed too, but he told me straight up that he wasn't doing anything else like that. Jab wasn't exactly a square nigga. He used to be part of a gang years back, but he paid his dues and got out before he got too caught up. Jab stayed to himself after getting away from the streets. He kicked it with his homies and shit like that. That was it though; he no longer roamed the streets. And from what he told me a few weeks back, he was set on moving to work on making his dreams a reality. Jab had the same dream so many other niggas had in the hood; making music in hopes that it would someday pay off.

"You sure don't play any games," Wayne spoke time I opened the door to his all-white Rolls Royce. He sat in the back smoking a cigar; his driver had his eyes focused ahead. Wayne didn't have to give the nigga any farther directions, he just pulled away from the parking space and was taking us to wherever the fuck we were heading. Talking to Wayne was supposed to be a brief meeting, not some half a day task. Jab had things to do aside from sitting inside of a warehouse holding Lyric hostage until I got back.

"I'm just a man of my words. I tell you I will come through and that's what I do best. You want the Eastside Warriors, you want to take all of Don's old locations and become the biggest honcho in the state. Your wish was my command." I slid my phone in my pocket after I shot Jab a brief message reminding him of what to do and not do. "But there's a slight change in the plans. I'm not going to serve as your right hand; I'm getting out."

"That wasn't part of the deal that we made, Osiris. You know that. If you're not there when I take over the team, they're not going to listen to me or swear their loyalty to my team. It would be bringing snakes into my camp. And once they find out 'bout Lyric, they will be in a rage," Wayne spoke with the cigar midway to his lips.

My decision was final; set in stone. Being a right hand to another man would only put me in another dire situation. Wayne and I hadn't been good friends over the years, and who's to say he didn't have a death wish planned out for my ass once he got the Eastside Warriors loyalty after using me as bait?

"You said you wanted them on your team; that the Warriors were yours for the taking. I gave you that. I made all that possible for you. They're yours once I finish removing Lyric out the way. I respect you, Wayne. I do. I trust you in a certain way too, but I can't serve as right hand anymore. I'll put a good word in for you to the Eastside Warriors, but that's all I will do." If the car wasn't moving, I would've ended the meeting and hopped out the car. "You can just let me out somewhere up the street since this isn't going anywhere. I can find my way back over to the place."

"Do you remember the detective friend I mentioned?" Wayne put his cigar out, folding his arms in the process.

"Yeah, but I did everything you told me. So, why bring him up?" Fear wasn't something any man on earth was able to put in my heart. I feared no muthafucka, because in the end we all had to die. None of us were immortal.

"Well, that's him driving the car," Wayne said through a light chuckle. My heart dropped to my ass. It felt like it grew fists, and was trying to beat its way out. It was a terrible feeling sitting inside of someone's car on the edge of a threat. If Wayne was stuck on doing business with me, I couldn't understand why the fuck there was a detective inside of the car with us to begin with.

"Okay. Hello Mr. Detective," I replied, frowning like I was being sprayed with pepper spray. "Do you think I'm supposed to be scared?"

"Naw, I don't expect you to be scared. You're fuckin' Osiris, the right hand to the Eastside Warriors. What the fuck do you have to fear?" Wayne said.

"Just let me out the car," I replied. Blowing Wayne's head off was only going to get me a sure murder charge. I decided against blowing a bullet through his dome again, because it was a mistake I knew that I would regret later. I was taught to shoot and think about it later. The years changed me, though. I was no longer that person. All I wanted was to keep a little peace for a while, until I got my army built.

"I don't think you understand me. Detective Samson read him his rights because he don't understand." Wayne kept his eyes on me. This had to be a big ass joke. It was no way a man like Wayne had gone through all that trouble just to incriminate me when he had unlawful deeds stacked on top of him.

"You have the right to remain silent…" Detective Samson started reading my rights and there were a swan of cops cars in front of us when we came to a complete stop. It didn't seem real.

LEX

There were no cars parked in the parking lot of the warehouse. It gave off the impression that it was an old location or maybe just some building he brought her to after realizing it was vacant and didn't get any visitors. I told Beatz to stay in the car, but not seconds later, he was right behind me. He wanted to be there when we saved Lyric. He wanted to get in her good grace by playing the hero. He still had a lot to do to be back in my good grace. He was still at fault for Michael's death. The blood was still on his hands, although he made it clear those were not the orders he gave those clown ass niggas.

"You check the lower floor while I go upstairs. Make sure there's no one else here besides us. And take this. Use it, and please shoot to kill." I tossed a Glock 19 to Beatz, praying like hell he didn't let me down.

"Shoot to kill? I thought we weren't here to hurt anybody?" Beatz's whispers echoed slightly through the warehouse so light, it resembled a gust of wind slow dancing in the air.

"If you want to live, you'll shoot and figure it out later. Unless you want them to place a bullet through your square ass brain," I said as I walked up the stairs. My gun was drawn back, ready for any nigga who wanted to jump out at me.

I checked the first few rooms upstairs and there wasn't a sign of a living soul. I was so close to yelling Lyric's name out, but that was some white people movie shit that would lead to my death. When I got to the last room on the list, the blood in my hands went cold. If I were lighter, they probably would've went white around the edges.

I heard a voice whispering then it was a full outburst of yelling. I held my Glock a bit tighter than before; so tight, it felt like my hands were blistering.

I wrapped my free hand around the doorknob and busted in the room. I fired a shot at the first man that I saw.

"Lyric." I sprinted over to where she was tied up. She looked the same, minus the bruises on her face and the fact that she was washed down in sweat, due to the heat inside of the building. If Osiris wasn't planning to shoot her, he was sure as hell planning to make sure she died from the heat.

"Lex." Lyric busted into tears. The man that was fighting for his life on the floor was begging me for help. I saw him on the block a few times. I believe I saw him and Osiris kicking it on a porch a few times over the years. If I wasn't mistaking, I remember somebody telling me that they were cousins. His life wasn't more important than Lyric's. I went there with the mindset to shoot to kill and that's exactly what I did. I learned a lot over the years from Pop; life lessons I would live out until my dying day. He didn't have to be the best example of a man to us, but there were skills he instilled in us that would get us through life without suffering at anyone's hand. And the whole Osiris situation taught me to never trust anybody who wasn't down since the beginning. Because even friends can turn to foes, and your lover your worst enemy.

I cut the zip ties and rope from around Lyric's arms, then I freed her legs. When she stood from the chair, she collapsed. Her body dropped right to the floor, helpless.

"Lyric." Beatz rushed into the room like he had an army behind him. "Is she alright? Did he hurt her?"

"Just call for help. Can you calm down and do that?" I shouted at Beatz. With all the things that took place in such a short amount of time, I learned how to get myself through it. I learned quick that being calm went a long way. Because if everybody was upset and panicking, things would turn from bad to worse in a matter of seconds.

"Okay." Beatz struggled to get his phone out his back pocket, tossing the gun on the floor like an idiot. If the man on the floor got ahold of the gun, we all probably would've been blasted.

I quickly retrieved the Glock that Beatz irresponsibly tossed to the floor, then went over to the man to see if he was strapped or not. That should've been the first thing I did before untying Lyric. That's how bitches in movies got knocked upside the head or a hole through the heart. Shit, it happened in real life in the hood. Being caught slipping was a huge mistake. A mistake that caused people to meet the grave.

"Please, I don't want to die. I wasn't going to hurt—" the man fell in silence as blood spilled from the inside of his mouth. When I fired a shot, I wasn't fully paying attention to the aim. I looked down at the blood that wouldn't let up. He had a gunshot wound to the left side of his chest; possibly in his heart. I turned a blind eye though, if he really wasn't trying to hurt Lyric, he played a part by being there. So, he got his end.

I searched to see if he was strapped or not, but the nigga didn't have any kind of weapon. He didn't have nothing on him but a half-smoked blunt and a cigarette lighter. All I could do was shake my head at the sad sight in front of me. The way he begged for his life, he couldn't have been part of Osiris' scheme for long.

"I'm sorry. There's nothing I can do," I whispered.

A few seconds later, I was back over to Lyric. I wasn't the strongest girl walking, but I wasn't weak either. I picked Lyric up hallway from the floor. Beatz took the time to assist me after he ended the call with emergency officials. We carried Lyric all the way down the stairs and out the warehouse before lowering her onto the ground. It was hot outside, but nothing compared to the inside of that warehouse.

With a bit of wind blowing, and Beatz and I trying to fan her, I knew we were making progress. I checked her pulse a few times, the way Momma taught us when we were small children. Momma's dream was to become a nurse. She even went to school for it back in the day, then she settled into Pop's arms and let her dreams go. However, that still didn't stop her from teaching us a thing or two about how to save someone's life.

"What's that white stuff coming out of her mouth?" Beatz asked.

"Shit," I said, making sure I stayed calm. I positioned Lyric on her side. Judging from the white foam that was oozing from her mouth and the way her body started jerking, it was a sure sign of a seizure.

"Fuck, fuck, fuck!" Beatz was in a panic again for the second time in one day.

"You really need to calm down. Breathe," I said. I had been calm all day, but I was close to throwing the towel in and breaking down too. The only thing that kept me from losing my mind out there was the sound of the emergency vehicles approaching in the distance. I was able to breathe in a breath of fresh air for once in a long ass time. My sister wasn't going to die. Not there and not the fuck on my watch.

* * *

"Is she okay? Is Lyric okay?" Momma grabbed me the moment she was next to me. She was meaning to fall into my arms, but instead, I fell into hers. I needed her there. It was refreshing to see someone who meant the world to me there in the flesh.

"I don't know." I finally broke down. Since we'd been in the hospital, everything had been hush-hush. A nurse or doctor hadn't been out to check on us in over an hour. My nerves were shot and Beatz wasn't making them any better. He'd been crying his eyes out. He was set on blaming himself for it. He told me that if he tried harder, Lyric would still be his and she wouldn't be facing any of the things she was facing. That it would've been different. I wanted to tell him that was the truth. It wasn't the truth, though. Life had a way of making a fool out of everybody.

"It's going to be alright." Momma's voice made the moment ten times better. And as much as I despised Pop, I wished he was there that day, too. For him to go make the bitch ass nigga responsible pay the highest price by losing his life.

"I'm just so worried." Being in Momma's arms made it clear that although I was tough and had a violent heart, I had a soft side, too. There was a part of me that really cared about things; that cared about my family in ways that would make me light a fire to a nigga or bitch's ass about them. If Osiris wasn't already in hiding, then I prayed he would be, because I was coming for his ass with all the power and hatred in my fucking heart. The one trait I knew I got from Pop was the ability to hold a grudge and get back at people who wronged me. Osiris was going to meet my wrath real soon. He was about to get to know just how cold my heart could be towards a person who crossed me and my family. I was going to get my revenge for Pop and for Lyric. And when he was in my hands, it wasn't going to be a peaceful death either. The bitch as nigga was going to pay in the worse way.

"I know, baby. I am too, but we have to be strong." Momma released me after about five minutes. Both of our faces were mess. Boni was sitting in the chair farthest to the entrance door with her head down. With all the shit our family faced, I wasn't sure how much damage had been done to Boni. It broke my heart down to the core that it was probably going to take years just to get all our lives back on track.

LYRIC

I woke with tubes in my nose and an IV in my right arm along with a heart monitor. The room was white as fuck. It took me a moment to process everything. The last thing I remembered before waking was Lex untying me back at the warehouse then everything went black. It was lights out for me. There were no dreams; no afterlife experience that some people claim to have when they're near death. It was all black. No visits from Pop telling me to hold on, no angel in the midst trying to make me be less afraid. It was just black. One minute I was out, then the next, I woke in the hospital.

I removed the breathing tubes from my nose and sat upright on the bed. My eyes hurt and my chest was on fire. If I somehow died, I was in hell. My thoughts wouldn't even come together, no matter how bad I tried. They were everywhere. My mind was on Lex heavy though, and a sudden sickness crept into my stomach and worried me almost breathless. The thought of her dying back there in the warehouse trying to save me. If she was dead, I was going to give up on life altogether; just sit lonely in the dark and wait for death to consume me.

I grabbed hold onto the tall machine that I was attached to and stood to my feet. "Ouch." My legs were sore like I'd ran for miles at a time.

The door sprung open when I was approaching it. A man and a woman walked into the room in blue uniform. Obviously, one was a doctor while the other was a nurse. I hadn't gone to the hospital much throughout the years, but I knew how to put two and two together.

"Let's get you back in bed." The woman had a tight smile on her face. She probably fooled people around her easily, but she didn't have me fooled. She looked one smile away from losing her damn mind.

Once I was back in the bed, she checked the water levels in the IV bag, and placed the oxygen back over my nose. The whole time she was doing that, the man, who I guess was the doctor, was reading over papers attached to a clipboard.

"Alright, Ms. Cotton. I'm Doctor Lockhart. It's good to see you wake. You lost a lot of fluids from the environment you were in. You suffered from a heat stroke. And there are a few more things wrong." Doctor Lockhart flipped a page on the clipboard. He read over the page a bit before fixing his eyes on me. "According to the bloodwork we did yesterday, you're pregnant. We don't know how long yet, but you're pregnant. We have to do an ultrasound to see if the baby is okay."

I stared at him ready to see him break down in laughter while the joke was on me. Pregnant wasn't the kind of news an eighteen-year-old, who was figuring out life, was trying to hear. It especially wasn't the kind I wanted to hear after my boyfriend was on the nearing end of trying to kill me. He made sure he allowed me to suffer in the hot ass warehouse for what seemed like forever. I tried begging him, dropping all my pride to make it right and save my damn life. He refused to hear me out, though. He kept at what he was doing without a lick of remorse. There was no sadness in his eyes. Nothing at all.

"You have to be lying. I can't be pregnant. How am I pregnant?" I tried to get out the bed, but the pain I was feeling forced me to stay put.

"Do you know how babies are made Ms. Cotton?" Doctor Lockhart asked like I was a dumb ass teenager laying up there on the bed.

"I know how they are fuckin' made. I just can't be. This isn't… this isn't my life." Tears fell from my eyes through the screams. I suddenly felt lightheaded from the news. The urge to barf hit me at once. That's not how I was supposed to be living my life. I had a gang to run and all of my time was consumed with that. A baby didn't fit into that. "There has to be some kind of mix up."

"No Ms. Cotton. The results are accurate and we have to get an ultrasound done on you." Doctor Lockhart's words were muffled like he was underwater.

* * *

Momma, Lex and Boni came to pick me up from the hospital. It was just the three of us in the car with Lex behind the steering wheel as if she was a professional driver. I kept praying we made it home safely because she wasn't afraid to put the pedal to the metal. The whole way home, I was holding onto my seatbelt praying.

"I'm pregnant," I blurted out. When they were at the hospital visiting, I told the nurses to make sure they kept the news private. I had to be the one who broke it to them, and to let them know which choice I made concerning the pregnancy.

"What?" Momma and Lex said in unison. Lex almost swerved off the road when those words came out of my mouth.

"Yeah, and I'm going to keep it." Those words sounded stupider now that they were spoken in the universe. I didn't know a damn thing about raising a child. I helped Momma with Lex and Boni when they were little. It was going to be different than that, though, because I was going to be the primary caregiver, looking out for a small human as if my entire life was together.

"Who are you pregnant by?" Momma kept her head straight ahead when she asked me that question. According to the dates that were given, I knew exactly who the father was. I just had to figure out how to deal with that.

"I'll let you know in due time. Right now, I'm still trying to process all of this. I can't believe I was so damn reckless." I did enough crying when I was alone in the hospital. I forced myself to be strong.

"Having a baby isn't the end of the world. I can't say it's what I wanted for you since I know you have a bright future ahead of you, but it's not my decision to make for you. If you think having this baby is the right thing for you, then it's the right thing for you." Momma dropped the conversation with her final words about the situation and we all left it alone until I was ready to talk about it again.

From the hospital to our new place in Shreveport was only like fifteen minutes across the city. Living back in the neighborhood wasn't part of Momma's plan. She told me she didn't want to risk living in the hood anymore, although it was home for us for a long ass time. She and Pop grew up on that block and saw a lot of men and women come and go over the years. They gave back to the neighborhood, but since Pop wasn't there, she didn't feel safe being there without his protection, although the Eastside Warriors were for us.

When we pulled into the driveway, Beatz was standing near a black Honda Accord with balloons and a pink bag. He was the last person I wanted to see. He tried seeing me at the hospital a few times but I declined it. Lex kept telling me it was a good idea to see him and that it was him who practically saved my life.

"What is he doing here?" I looked at Lex then at Momma who was already exiting the car. Since everybody was getting out the car, I followed their lead. I made quick strides towards the door to give myself some distance from Beatz.

"Lyric, hold up. I just want to have a word with you." Beatz approached me with the familiar pureness. I hadn't realized how much I missed being next to him until I was back in his presence and knew he wasn't the one who put Pop down. "Please, just hear me out."

"Fine." I took a deep breath, trying to keep my temper under control.

"I'm sorry I wasn't what you needed. I saw you laughing in his face like you wanted to be with him at the Shoe Toss. Then you went on a date with him like we were nothing. Like our relationship didn't mean a damn thing to you. It hurt me to the core. I didn't know how to deal with it. So, I took T-Max up on the offer to be the honcho of the 211s. Then I started plotting against Don for petty reasons. Mostly because he didn't see me as being enough for you. But I promise you, it was never my intention for anybody to get hurt." Beatz said all those words in one breath with tears running down his face. There weren't a lot of men I knew who was open about their feelings the way he was. I never saw Pop cry when he was in the wrong when he and Momma had it out and she threatened to leave for the hundredth time. What Beatz did was stupid, but it was all out of temporary feelings. Something he would forever regret until he learned to let it all go.

"Thank you for helping Lex find me. I guess it's a start of me learning to forgive you." I accepted the balloons and gifts.

"Lyric, I promise I won't fold on you again. Just give me another chance. Please, I will do anything." Beatz's face was messy with tears. And to see the bruises on his face inflicted by Osiris made guilt rise to my throat. To know I was allowing the man who was really responsible for killing Pop inflict pain on another person who meant the world to me, regardless of how bad things were between us.

"I hope you don't. I really hope you live up to those words since you're going to be a dad." Those words didn't even seem right.

"What? What are you talking about?" Beatz asked. His face was red like cayenne. If I were him, it would sound suspect to me, too because we used protection all the time. However, we had like three incidents where the condom popped. And if the doctor didn't give me the dates and confirmed how far along I was, I would've believed the baby belonged to Osiris.

"Yeah, I'm pregnant and I'm sure it belongs to you. We can still do the whole DNA test thing to be sure, but I have no doubt that this baby belongs to you." I broke down in tears in front of Beatz. To think the whole time we were at war with each other I was carrying his baby made sorrow drown my heart. Although what we shared was suffering, due to hurt, we were going to find a way to make it through all of it.

"Lyric. Oh my god. This is-this is great. I don't know a damn thing about being a dad but I will still be the best that I can be." Beatz picked me up in his arms and he kissed me. It all felt right, like this was supposed to be for us since the beginning.

Time he let me down, I heard a car bend the block and bullets started rippling. I took cover the best I could until the gunfire stopped. When the car finally sped away, I ran out there next to Beatz in a panic. He had been hit. My best friend, my lover, my child's father was in the yard fighting for his life.

"Helpppppp," I screamed. During the fear of losing him, I realized I loved him with the last breath in me.

LYRIC

The bullets, the smell of gunpowder, all the commotion brought me back to the day that I lost my pop. The confusion drowned me, wrapped me in a thick wave and carried me to sea. That day wasn't supposed to happen that way. When the doctors released me after staying for a few days, I was set on getting home and trying to cope with my new reality. The bittersweet reality of fast-approaching motherhood. One car filled with a bucket of rage bent the block and opened fire on the man that loved.

"Momma, help! Help me!" Tears were so thick in my eyes, everything around me was blurred.

When I made the deal with 211 Vipers, I made sure to notify everyone that Beatz wasn't to be touched, then when the truth came out, I knew there wasn't anything to worry about because the target was no doubt on Osiris. Osiris was the one who put an end to the Eastside Warriors' OG. He was to blame for Pop being dropped; he was the muthafucka behind the gun. All hell was supposed to come down on his ass.

Somewhere in the middle of me having a nervous breakdown, Momma ran out of the house with Lex right behind her. Momma dropped right to her knees to perform first aid. She kept yelling out demands at Lex and for me to snap the fuck out of my trance. But I couldn't, I couldn't. I kept drifting.

"Ma, Lyric was hit too. Lyric was hit." I heard panic creep into Lex's throat and release through what seemed like a cry. I was hit!

* * *

WHEN I WOKE, Momma was sitting beside my bed. No one else was in the room, just me and Momma. My first instincts were to get the hell out that bed and see if Beatz was okay. He had to be okay. Facing another death would break my spirit and I wasn't sure what I was going to do from there. Beatz and I were close; he had my heart for the longest time, even when I was too naïve to see it for what it was. Then the whole thing with Osiris made me waiver. Temptation brought me to my knees and almost made me lose a friend that was dearest to me since I could remember.

"Lyric?" Momma closed the *Bible* that rested on her lap that I didn't notice before. "Thank God, you're up. I'm just happy he saw you through it. I was one second away from losing my mind."

"Where's Beatz? I need to see him, Momma." I tried to sit upright on the bed but the soreness in my stomach snatched me back like an abusive husband.

"Beatz is alright baby, it's just..." Momma took a moment to view me. Her eyes were welled with water. If I could move, if I was able to get my ass out that bed and wrap my arms around her that's what I would've done. "The doctor said you lost the baby due to being shot in the stomach. He said some medical talk for you to better understand how it happened. But yeah, you lost the baby."

I laid on the bed lost for words; I hadn't even known I was pregnant for a full week. And it was all snatched from me. Although Beatz and I had gone through the wringer, I was looking forward to starting over with a new life that we made together. The child was part of both of us. There was no doubt it was going to shake our lives up for the good and in some parts, the bad. But I was ready for all of that. At the tender age of eighteen, I was ready to be somebody's mother because I had a support system that was going to make sure everything went smooth.

"I'm sorry, baby. I'm so sorry." Momma broke down in a big sob that made my soul cry. That's all though, my soul cried while my eyes remained dry. I felt the sorrow swim around inside, nothing that was able to rise to the surface. "I want to question God so bad. But I know it's not my place. It's not my place to ask him why he took Don from me, why there's so many enemies after us and why, just why an unborn child had to suffer at the hand of our foes. It's not my place. He sits high and looks low. That's the only truth I know."

"It's okay. I'm fine. I just want to see Beatz," I said. Those words were farthest away from the truth than anything in life. Little by little, God was taking everything from me. I was paying for sins of my pop. Being punished for sins he committed long before God blew the breath of life through my nostrils. I wasn't the one to pull the trigger on innocent people. I just got back at the people who wronged me. At the people who posed as a threat to my family, that's how it was supposed to go. But I realized laying on that bed, the streets never stopped. Because when he offed one enemy, a dozen more surfaced. I would be watching my back until God decided to snatch my breath away.

"Lyric, it's okay to be hurt. It's okay. You don't have to be strong for any of us. You don't." Momma grabbed my hands and placed them in hers while her tears never let up. I still wasn't shedding any tears. I'd done enough crying over the last month. Enough of my tears were in the universe.

"I'm fine," I replied in a sharp tone. I just wanted to see Beatz and the rest of my life was going be figured out later down the road. He was still alive, we were still breathing. We had time to start a family again if that's what we wanted for our lives. I figured it was God's way of trying to teach me how to appreciate the things that didn't even seem like a blessing.

"Okay." Momma let it go. She never was the kind of person to keep pressing an issue when someone wanted to be left alone for their own good. That's what I adored about her. "Soon as you're all healed up you'll be able to see Beatz. Right now he's trying to recover just like you. Just heal up and you'll be back in his arms before you know it, Lyric."

"Yes, ma'am." I swallowed a ball of emotions right before it reached the surface. I kept thinking what Pop must've been going through all those years when all he wanted was good for the streets and the streets were an enemy to him. To find out that one of his own was a traitor would've ripped his emotions into pieces if he was alive to see it. I would've bet money on it. Because knowing how Osiris played two roles, troubled my soul. Made me want to drop hell on any nigga's head who I thought was a threat to my family. That's how the gang was supposed to go.

With Gates and Trever being dead and Osiris missing all the muthafuckin' action, there was nobody I knew who was ready to step up to be my right hand. That very reason had my mind in overdrive. I had 211s in my circle; they were in my circle while my team was falling to shits. I would've paid any price to visit Pop wherever he was to get his input on the situation. I was lost. I jumped in his role as honcho and had to hit the ground running or sink my ass to the bottom of the sea with the sharks. My family was depending on me, the fate of the Eastside was depending on me. I had to pull myself together regardless of all the trauma I experienced. It was my job to carry all the people who looked up to me. Pop did for the longest he was crowned honcho. He made decisions in favor of his people, decisions he knew would carry me through the years and that's what I had to wake up to realize. There was no more sparing niggas' lives or feeling sorry for them. If they made a hit at my team, my family, then I was coming for theirs locked and loaded.

"Lyric, did you hear me?" Momma's voice grabbed me back to the moment with her. I was so zoned out thinking on my next move, she was just a damn fly on the wall to the thoughts she wasn't able to hear.

"I'm sorry, what?" I looked over at her. I was disgusted with myself for being in the hospital again. I had just left the damn place. And laying in a hospital bed for the second time in under a month, I vowed to never lose the upper hand again. My enemies were going to bow before me.

"They have Osiris in custody," Momma laid those words on me like I would be happy. Naw, Osiris shouldn't have had the privilege of being behind bars for any of his crimes. I wanted him to face me and my team. Make him suffer for his crimes until he understood his treason, then I would put an end to his suffering after he admitted to his wrongful deeds.

"In custody, since when did the cops get involved with all this shit?" I asked.

"Can I be completely honest with you, Lyric?" Momma leaned forward in the chair with her eyes fixed on me. The look she gave me was like a stranger was sitting in the room. I saw my momma face a lot of things, I was a witness to all the things she'd been through. But I hadn't ever seen that kind of expression on her face.

"What?" The word flew out of my mouth without any proceeding words. I just wanted her to get down to whatever the hell she had to lay on me. After dealing with all the bullshit I'd faced, nothing was going to come as one big surprise to me anymore. In the short few weeks I'd been running things, I swear I had seen it all. Everything in the honcho handbook had been before my eyes. It made to grow some thick ass skin too.

"Wayne had always been a genuine man to me, Lyric. Always. And I know all of this, this gang stuff was getting the better of you. So, I handed it over to him. It's his team now and you can go do whatever you please. He told me that long as I relinquish the gang to him that he will get any and everybody who wronged our family." Momma sounded crazy as hell sitting in that chair. She had no fucking power to make a decision like that. She wasn't some leading lady of the damn Eastside Warriors. Pop never let her in on his business, but she thought she could undermine me and give my team over to a nigga who didn't even have my damn trust. That's not how I got down and never would. Momma had a whole lot of learning to do.

"You don't even know Wayne from a can of paint. You don't know shit about this gang shit or what comes with the territory. While Pop was running the streets, you were in the house making pies and shit. Stepping in this is dangerous and what you did will not fly with me. This is my crew. The Eastside Warriors are mine…it's our family's lifeline. You think Wayne cares that much to come to our rescue if we lose our team and the streets come after us? You have another thing coming." My head was hurting laying in that bed. I couldn't believe my momma could be so stupid to make a deal with Wayne. A fucking deal she couldn't even deliver.

OSIRIS

Sitting in that cell the day Wayne crossed me kept repeating. I let my guard down and trusted the nigga. I went against all my teachings that Don taught me, learning from all his damn mistakes, only to drop the ball and allow a nigga like Wayne to cross me. He made me look like a damn fool on the streets. I was the one to bring Don to his grave but wasn't smart enough to keep myself in the clear of going to prison. They had footage; all the evidence was there. I slipped up and forgot about all the damn cameras outside of the hotel; I put myself in a bad position. I knew my Mom Duke was shaking her head while looking down at my ass. Prison was the last place I needed to be. Don had a few niggas serving time on his behalf out of loyalty, and I was sure they would try to bash my head in the moment I stepped foot in the same prison as them.

"Smalls," I heard the approaching guard. Those clown ass cops kept coming next to my cell laughing in my face and shit. They kept threatening me about who they had on the inside and that I was low down for dropping Don like that. I wasn't any stranger to the weight Don's name carried out there, I just never expected the cops to be open about their grief. They were really set on getting my ass murdered behind those bars.

The cell door opened and instead of placing handcuffs on me, they allowed me to walk free of any restraints. If I tried something, it wasn't like I could get out that bitch alive when they had niggas strapped from the front door all the way to the back.

"That's treason nigga," I heard an inmate yell from one of the cells. I wasn't afraid to face any of those niggas in there and wasn't going to bow down to anybody. "You gon' get banished nigga. Eastsideeeeee!" I wasn't even in prison yet and niggas locked up in the jail were already making their set known.

"Aye, shut up." The guard hit his baton against the bars. The sounded echoed across the building and the yells suddenly stopped.

"Am I meeting my lawyer? Because I told them, I'm not speaking unless my lawyer is in the room," I said. One second I was speaking my rights then the next I was hit across the face with a baton.

"I don't think you understand; you don't run the show up in here." The guard kept walking. I had to force myself to stay on his heels to keep from falling to the floor. My face instantly felt like it was swelling after that blow. Blood was dripping onto the concrete floor, drops staining the already stained floor. I wanted to beat his fucking head in for doing some shit like that. I was somebody out there and they were treating me like I was nothing and no one.

After walking for what seemed like hours, we were finally approaching a room that was isolated from the rest of the facility. I'd heard horror stories about what those pigs did to niggas behind bars; treated us all the same. It wasn't any race thing; it was just street niggas against the niggas behind the badges. They thought they were bad because they hid behind a badge and a gun. Let the streets out though and we would win every time in a fair fight.

When I walked into the room there were two white niggas sitting at the desk and the black ass detective nigga who was with Wayne in the car. The supposed driver. I believe his name was Samson or some weak-ass name. Seeing his face in there made my blood boil ten times over.

"Osiris, good to see you still alive." Detective Samson was the first one to open his mouth to speak to me. The smug ass smirk on his face irked the life in me.

"What is that supposed to mean?" I looked around at every one of them in the room. I was outnumbered one to four and they had guns ready to blow my ass away on the first sign of trying to off them.

"It means, it's good to see you alive since everybody and they momma wants to end your dumb ass. You have to be the dumbest nigga walking to pull some shit like that," Detective Samson said through a light chuckle. "But on another note, a more serious note. Do you know anyone by the name of Young Dro?"

"I told y'all before I have rights and I refuse to speak without a lawyer being present," I said sternly. Detective Samson looked around the room at each man before he did some kind of hand gesture to the man who brought me into the room.

The guard slammed the baton against both sides of my ribs with every intention to shatter them. I fell to the floor and balled up as he continued to beat me without any sign of letting up. He kept at what he was doing, slamming his baton against my back, my head and against my ribs four more times before Detective Samson called him off. I hadn't ever been so happy to hear those words. I wanted to thank him, although he was the one who was the cause of the bitch ass cop beating on me like that.

"Now, do you understand we're not here to play any damn games?" Detective Samson pulled me up from the floor like I was a piece of paper. I wasn't some tall nigga; he had me by at least four or more inches and looked like he lived inside of the gym. He wasn't the ordinary detective type nigga.

"Understood." I knew that if I wanted to get my ass out the mess that I caused for myself then I had to abide by their rules and forget about my rights. They weren't the kind of cops who were following the law; they worked under the table. And sitting there, I knew they had a hand in the streets.

"Now who is Young Dro?" Detective Samson asked.

"I don't really know him like that. All I know is that he wanted to do business with Don but Don wasn't having it. He was too comfortable in the way he lived to be making deals with niggas who he didn't know. So, I respected that and never got back in contact with the nigga," I spoke my truth. About the only truth that didn't hurt me to tell. Young Dro was a stranger to me just like he was to them. He had no kind of involvements with him, and they would be a fool if they thought I would tell them any kind of truth that would farther incriminate me. "The nigga stationed out in Atlanta, what could you possibly want him?"

"That's for me to deal with but I want to use you as a pawn. He kind of knows you and you're kind of familiar with him. You just follow all the directions I give you and if you come through, I just might know someone who can get you out of this hot water that you boiled for yourself." Detective Samson was standing up there really offering me a deal. It made me want to nut up, because it was then that I realized, I wasn't there on any charges anyway. They wanted to use that murder over my head to make me do as I was told. And if I went against them, then and only then would I be serving my time for the murder of Don.

"Just like that?" I was slouched over my knees with pain overtaking my soul. The shit hurt me to the core.

"Just like that." Detective Samson shot a smug smirk at me. A crooked cop was the worst kind of person to cross; they had connections everywhere and could get out of just about anything. He excused the other men out the room, leaving just me and the one guard who'd been present the entire time. "And I hate to be the one to break it to you, but your cousin died yesterday after fighting for his life for days." Those words went straight through me. I heard what the hell he said. I had a hard time believing them as the truth. Jab didn't have anything to do with what I had going on. He was there making sure Lyric didn't escape, not to fucking harm her. He had his life ahead of him, prepared to move on to bigger and better things. It was because of me that his parents were going to bury their son. I played a role in him losing his life. It was my damn fault that Jab didn't get a chance to get out the fucking hood how he wanted. His blood was going to forever be on my hands. I pulled him into all that bullshit.

"Naw, naw. See that can't be right. He can't be dead. You understand? He had his whole life ahead of him. He was going to make it out. He was supposed to make it out of this town…away from all of this." All of a sudden, the pain went away and I was once again filled with rage like all the other times when I faced spiritual pain. Jab was the only nigga who really knew me. He told me that he didn't feel right being there, that he had a bad feeling that day. And I just brushed him off and told him he was being a pussy. It was my damn fault. I should've been the one there when that shot was fired. If anybody deserved a bullet, it was me. "He can't be dead!"

"I thought thugs didn't have heart." Detective Samson walked out the room with his same dirty ass smirk. Wasn't shit funny though; a good ass person had lost his life at my hand. Fuck all the lives I took, he wasn't the one who deserved it.

* * *

AFTER A WEEK of being inside of that shitty ass place and getting the life beat out of me, I was walking out of those doors just in time for Jab's funeral. I had been going to funerals left and right. I was losing all the people closest to me and it made me think back on all the damn pain I caused Lyric. I had every intention to kill her. Because that's how the game went, we didn't have pity on our hearts for people who would turn around and off us in the end. She knew too much, accused me of too much. I couldn't trust her anymore, even if I had feelings for her.

"Are you woke now?" Oisin sat next to me in the church. His words still didn't mean a damn thing though. No matter what, I belonged to the streets and the thug life until my dying day. I couldn't walk my rough around the edges ass in a building to interview for a job. I would be torturing myself with that kind of foolery.

"Naw, I'm still sleeping," I said. Nobody's tragedy was going to make me run for the hills. I was built for street life. I didn't choose the streets, the streets chose me. "And I would appreciate if you just focused on the service. Give some respect, bruh." I turned my attention back to the preacher. And right behind him, I glimpsed a shadow. A shadow that was so familiar my heart stopped beating for a second. It was a moment I would never forget.

LEX

It hurt my soul to know all the shit Lyric was facing. She wasn't the happiest person when she broke the news about being pregnant. I knew she was taking it kind of hard though since losing something that was part of her, regardless of how the situation came about. I had to give it to her though. Even after all the shit she went through, she was still set on making moves in the town. Making changes in our hood. And hell, with her decision we were getting a house rebuilt in place of our new one. We could've gone anywhere in the world of our choosing but we agreed to go back to the place Pop ordained as our stomping ground. Eastside would always be our home until our names were washed away from the streets.

However, with all the shit that was going on, Lyric needed someone to stand by her side as her right hand, and I stepped my young ass up. I couldn't care less about how people felt seeing us run the team as a duo. Our pops lived and breathed through the Eastside Warriors; their loyalty now belonged to us. And with Lyric being out of the hospital along with Beatz, we had some shit to get straight. The 211s rightfully belonged to Beatz and although he didn't want any parts of the streets, he had a hand to play in it because there was no one we would relinquish our hand to be stomped on out there.

"I need to know who's down for us and who's here to cause problems? We don't have time placing our trust in niggas who only want to off us." I walked around the room; I was trying to read niggas' souls like I saw Pop do once back at the warehouse the night we were fleeing for our lives. Not even knowing our real enemy was the one he placed to protect us. Pop was grilling a whole lot of niggas that night, not knowing his own right hand was out to get him and wasn't going to stop until he was dead. "Who down for the fuckin' Eastside?" The entire building fell into yells then turned it into the chant of the Eastside Warriors. We weren't going to let our side of the town die. Our team would live on through us and hopefully the generations after us would still keep our legacies alive.

"As you all know, Osiris is no longer serving as the right hand to the Eastside Warriors after being found guilty in the murder of Pop. And he had three niggas who were down with him, two of them I had to take care of by myself while he offed the other one. I knew to step up came along with all kinds of challenges, but I'm here to stay. We're here to stay and I refuse to give up my seat for the next nigga." Lyric sat in the chair across the room. A big ass chair that was rightful for a princess like her. She was still recovering from being shot down and losing her child, but there she sat in the middle of the team showing them that she was strong and worthy of their loyalty. "I'm standing on my word today and forever: I will not tolerate anybody trying to cross me. I will not lose another member of my family or my team due to disloyalty. If you're not for us then be against us and go to another team. I swear there will not be any hard feelings."

I looked around the room, trying to see if a nigga let off the wrong type of vibe in there. Lyric was about letting them out freely. That was her though, it was her thing. She wanted them to be able to put up a fair fight, so relinquishing to another team was her way of setting them up to be destroyed. But I, on the other hand, wasn't for all that fair bullshit. The moment someone stepped out the line in the building to show their true colors, I was going to place a bullet in their dome. It was the only way I saw it. Allowing more known enemies to lurk amongst us was only digging our graves. And I wasn't planning on dying any time soon due to us making a stupid-ass decisions out of fairness. The streets weren't fair and niggas who lived by the streets and the code of the streets didn't give a damn about being fair to anybody who posed as a threat to them. It's how shit went out there. And it was how we were going to operate.

"Does anybody want to fucking walk?" I yelled from the top of my lungs. I had to give it to myself. I didn't sound like some child throwing a tantrum. I sounded like a whole damn gangsta in there.

"I'm down for the team. Don was like a father figure to a lot of us in here. I don't know about all these niggas in here, but I grew up on the block looking up to that nigga. Admiring all the shit he did for the hood over the years. He was my fuckin' dad when my own dad didn't want a damn thing to do with me. I'm ridding for the Eastside." Dre put his fist in the air and the rest of the Warriors that stood in the room followed his lead.

"Then let's get these streets back under control. Let's find the niggas who shot Lyric and Beatz and let's take back over these muthafuckin' streets." I placed my fist in the air too and we all stood like that for a moment. We showed each other that we were a team. We were family and family stuck together even when the walls were closing in on them. "We are a family. We are built for all the trials life is throwing at us."

"Family," everybody said in unison. It felt good standing in there, making Pop proud, although we didn't see eye to eye when he was alive. I knew he had to be looking down at both Lyric and me proud that the streets didn't fold us. That it was unable to get underneath our skin. We were built for the life of crime.

* * *

"You were good in there." Lyric struggled to her feet from the desk chair. She'd been struggling with the simplest tasks all day, and seeing her struggle shattered my heart. "Pop would be proud to see you having a hand in all of this. Never think he didn't love you, because he did. He just dealt with things differently than a lot of people. You know he sometimes spent a lot of time on the wrong thing while abandoning the things or people who needed his attention the most." Lyric's words arrived out of nowhere. They touched my soul though; I'd been walking around dealing with things my own way by doing things that Pop wouldn't have approved. But deep down my soul was still mourning. I kept thinking back on what he must've thought of me when I pulled that gun on him and how broken I was that he had ruled me as his enemy. His life was taken before we could even have a talk and stand on mutual grounds. He was stubborn when it came down to stating he was in the wrong and so was I.

"Thank you." I wrapped my arms around Lyric, holding her in a light embrace. Having my sister in my life, I wasn't ever in need of a best friend. My sister knew all there was to know about me. We argued and sometimes didn't see eye to eye, but our love for each other was never in question. She was my heart and with both of us fighting for the same cause, we were going to be on top. Ruling the hood as Pop did over the years.

"No, need to thank me. It's the truth." Lyric broke into a slight sob, and I joined her. We had faced a lot of things together and were going to rise from all of the mistakes and lessons learned during those tribulations.

"I'll be home later." I finally released Lyric from my embrace. Qbaby invited me to a house party they were having on the Eastside at one of his homie's spot. And since I didn't have anybody telling me I couldn't go or that it was a bad idea, I agreed to show. Plus, anybody that was somebody was going to be there. They even invited Lyric and Beatz to show their faces to put on a show for the party, but they were still recovering after almost losing their lives.

"Be safe out there, and just because Pop ain't here, don't be letting no lil' nigga push up all on you like that either. You keep to yourself and get one of your friends to go with you. And I know, I know you can handle your own but I'm sending Dre with you. For your protection," Lyric said. I guess I had spoken too damn soon because Lyric sounded like Pop reloaded. She wanted to make sure I had somebody watching over me and that I wasn't just in the spot alone. Dre was a familiar face, wasn't high rank when Pop was ruling the gang but he was somebody trustworthy from the way Lyric was giving him orders and trusting him with things she didn't trust anyone else with.

"Just when I thought I truly had freedom," I said.

"You do have freedom, but your freedom comes with protection. I will not lose another person that I love. Lex, I never saw it before, but I see it now. We have a lot of enemies out there as well as loyal members who will lay their lives down for us. But sometimes foes have a way of sneaking in and going in for the kill." Lyric looked at me for a moment before continuing with what she had to say. "Don't trust anybody."

"Okay, I understand. I got you, sis. I'll make sure I stay on my tens," I said. I couldn't call a friend to go with me because all my friends were probably doing their own thing. And Moomoo and I weren't getting along. She had feelings for me, feelings that I didn't have in my heart for her. I told her that she was a good person and that somebody would be happy to be with her in that kind of way. I just wasn't that person and never would be. That was something she was going to have to realize if she wanted to rekindle our friendship. However, since I' wasn't the one to mess things up between us, I refused to be the one to be the bigger person.

"Good, and no staying overnight anywhere. You will report back home after the party," Lyric said sternly. Her mentioning me not spending the night anywhere let me know that she got word on me staying overnight at Qbaby's spot.

"Okay, understood." I headed to the door. I adored the fact that she cared about me and she didn't want any harm coming to me. It was a good feeling to know that I had someone in my corner that cared for me as Pop did. We were both looking out for each other and our family. Even with the dumb ass mess Momma got herself in with Wayne, we still were looking out for her the best we knew how. Because sometimes family disappointed one another but still, they stuck it out regardless and made it work. That was the kind of family I always wanted to be part of.

"And watch your back with him," Lyric made sure she spoke those very words as I walked out. I knew little about Qbaby; he was older than me. But Lyric, she heard of a lot of people since she was older than me. She went to school with a lot of the niggas on the block. Some she watched drop out before graduation was near while others she stood beside at graduation.

"Lyric, I got this. Just chill. Besides, I know how to shoot a nigga in the nuts if he tries some fuck shit." I let out a light giggle and continued on my way out the door. Lyric must have already spoken to Dre because he was already on my heels like a bloodhound.

BEATZ

"What's the matter?" Lyric asked while she sat on the bed. It felt strange being in there with her after all the things we went through. That day I apologized, I didn't think she would find it in her heart to forgive or lay news on me that she was pregnant with my child. A child that was taken from us before we could bask in futures plans surrounding it. It was the moment that was bittersweet and vanished like the snow in the south after falling the night before.

"You changed in so many ways. And I don't mean that as a bad thing. You know I grew up being around you, hearing you out and all that. You're stronger now. You've been through so much but you're still walking around here with your head leveled on your shoulders. It's a really beautiful thing to see, Lyric." I made my way over to her. She was everything I'd ever wanted, and still to that day I wanted to beat my ass for turning against her like that. Even if she was feeling somebody else, I should've put my feelings aside and still been there for her. When she pushed me off that day, it was my job to show her why I was essential in her circle. We were meant to be with each other in some way.

"I wish I could take credit for all of that. But see, the truth is that I've been losing my damn mind. I thought about throwing in the towel so many times. Because I felt like a big ass joke to my team. And it was already bad that you played a part in some of the things…I forgave you though. I did. Then to know that the man I walked away from you for was the man who was plotting against my dad, it broke something in me," Lyric said those words as she looked down at the floor. I was always able to tell when it was hurting someone to express themselves by their body language. "Then after all of that, I find out that I'm carrying a baby. A baby, Beatz. I was scared, confused and a bit disappointed. But that child was part of me, so I decided to keep it. Then just like that, just like that it was snatched from me. From us." Lyric finally looked up to me and her face was a mess. I'd seen Lyric cry a few times in the past, held her through some of her pain over the years. Noting how I saw her sitting on that bed though, she was broken, a broken person who was good at appearing strong to the public, hell the people closest to her too.

"Lyric, it's okay. You're going to be just fine. I think it's still beautiful that you haven't folded, you wanted to, but you didn't. And if I can go back and change all the things you've been through I would in a fuckin' heartbeat." Lyric and I were both at our end. She was busy trying to make sure I was straight while not realizing she'd been hit too. While I was in the hospital recovering, all I could think about was holding Lyric in my arms after what felt like years. I just wanted to be next to her at all cost. Put my life on the line for her to live.

"I love you, Rashad. I really do. And I can't believe I chose someone else over you. I was naïve, thinking that's the kind of man that I needed because of what my Pop wanted. He didn't approve of you. I thought I loved Osiris at one point. That I had fallen for him. When all along my heart still belonged to you." Lyric wiped away tear after tear. I could no longer suffer to watch her cry; we were both still in pain but I sat on the bed next to her and I wrapped my arm around her and we both laid back on the bed like old times. Just looking at the ceiling fan go around and around until we both fell into a slumber. It was nights like that that made life worth living.

* * *

SINCE WE'D BEEN RELEASED from the hospital, Lyric was set on making sure she had the right people on her team. She had been having meetings all damn week back to back. Some niggas she banished from the team; it was an executive decision that had to be made. It was mostly the new niggas. And with me on her side, the 211 Vipers were ready to work with and for her. It was the respect they had for me and the men in my family before me. With Lyric agreeing to bring T-Max back, all the 211s were happy as fuck for what the new team and management had to offer. T-Max wasn't going to be the right hand to the Eastside Warriors; instead, he was going to be just an advisor who looked out for our best interest. He didn't argue with that either; he was happy to be back in town and around the people who were known as his family. I was just pleased I was able to work something out with Lyric to get him back. Because with all the things we faced, we needed somebody that we were really able to trust through all of it.

"I don't know how you pulled that off but thank for getting me back here. I was one day away from losing my damn mind. Just one damn day." T-Max grabbed me in a brotherly embrace. It felt good him being back in town. He was the reason hands down that I got caught up in gang shit in the first place; however, he was the first man that took time out with me over the years and stepped up to something like a father figure. My dad was doing life on a sentence, and my momma made sure she made it clear I was to never go see him. He wrote letters all the time, letters that I never opened. I put them all in a stash until I was ready to open them. No matter what the letters said or how much he regretted his decisions in life, words couldn't make up for my childhood without having a dad in my life. He couldn't step away for one damn second to think about me or his other supposed son.

"I think it was always meant to go this way you know. To teach all of us something. I know I won't regret not one second of being with Lyric. Never again," I said.

T-Max released me from the embrace, he viewed me for a good minute then said, "I sure hope now you use this time to get on your shit for real this time. No holding back. Take over these streets and have the entire hood bumping yo' shit. You got talent and a whole lot of damn heart."

"You already know I'm working on something. I want to get Lyric back on her shit too. We can do this once and for all. I'll be ready for whatever comes after all the hard work," I replied. Music was the one thing that brought Lyric and I together after all those years. Our life was one big Hip Hop show without all the damn fans. Our lives came along with drama, seeing niggas dropped on the streets, being shot at and love. We were the artists but our lives were the real story.

"Then do that. I know I was set on you being the honcho of the 211s, that I wanted you to put them first. But just know there's always a way out of this, young nigga. If doors to your dreams start knocking, you go chase them. You don't want to be an old man like me still on the same path." Those were the realest words I'd ever heard someone speak. T-Max never was the type to sugarcoat anything. The events that manifested were all for our better good. Judging from T-Max's words, he'd grown in some areas.

"Thank you for that." I ended the conversation with that and left it alone. We both had a better understanding of each other. T-Max knew it was music that kept me alive and I knew the streets were the air he breathed and I respected his drive to stay loyal all those years. T-Max stayed ten toes down with his team until he had to make a decision for the better, a decision to keep his men alive because they were about to be shoved in the corner by the Eastside Warriors. He made a decision not knowing that it was the decision that would reunite everybody as one big family and that their loyalty was stronger than ever. Lyric had somehow formed a brotherhood that not even Don or any of the honchos over the 211s ever could do. They were working together under the same roof. The Southside and Eastside had a brotherhood, a brotherhood that never existed in street history until then. All thanks to Lyric.

"You know they let him walk? Something about bringing down Young Dro's crew. Word on the street is that Young Dro wants to do business with Lyric, which has Wayne's thongs in a bunch. So, he's working with his detective friends to bring the nigga's crew to the ground. But they have Osiris to do all their dirty work." I swear T-Max knew more news than anybody I knew. He could be thousands of miles away and still hear what's going on with other crews. He had friends in all kind of places and wasn't a honcho. There were people who swore their loyalty to him. "Because you know Young Dro's crew is one of the crews who were in alliance with the 211s before we united with the Eastside Warriors. But words have been, he's been trying to be in business with the Eastside Warriors long before Don was killed."

"They let him go just like that. You know it's not safe for any of us since that nigga is walking the streets free. He has it out for Lyric and for me. Osiris won't be satisfied until we're all dead." I heard all the other shit T-Max laid on me, but I was more focused on the Osiris situation. I couldn't care less about a Young Dro and his team or what the cops and Wayne were trying to do with him. Osiris was out for blood. I knew he was going to come knocking eventually, I just had to make sure I was there to blow his head clean off his shoulders. That I was there to protect Lyric at all cost. His position was snatched from under his feet, the niggas he had in the circle that were working for him, were banished. Lyric made sure of it. He was coming for her. I felt that shit down in my bones.

"Look, we ain't gon worry 'bout no Osiris. The nigga doesn't have a team like we do. How do you think he's even going to make a hit for any of us? With the 211s and Eastside Warriors on the same team, our gang is the biggest in the state right now. We can't be fucked with," T-max said those words with every lick of confidence. He made me believe too that we were untouchable. The streets were about to hear about us.

"I just think *somebody* should get him before he comes for us. You see what I'm saying?" T-Max and I exchanged a mutual stare. We were on the same page without a doubt and Osiris was going to be seeing his end sooner rather than fucking later.

"I see what you're saying, baby savage. I peep that shit." T-Max reached out to shake my hand then we parted ways. Knowing the man that T-Max was, he was going to handle things that needed to be handled.

LYRIC

"This is for all the people who lost somebody or are going through the struggle. Remember to hold your head up and keep that chest poked out. It gets better." I removed the headphones after recording the intro. It felt like old times, except I wasn't in Beatz's studio, we were in my bedroom recording new music. He had been on my ass all week about getting back on my grind and how I didn't have to give up on my dreams while leading the team. He made it clear that T-Max would keep me up to speed on everything. I had to give it to T-Max too, he knew way more shit about the streets than Osiris, which made me wonder why the hell he never decided to establish his own gang.

"That was hot. You know I can actually feel that you 'bout to drop fire ass lyrics after that intro." Beatz messed around with the computer for a minute. We were back in our usual elements. Before I faced the worst days of my life, I was only rapping about shit I heard people say they went through. But that night I was able to rap about my own life experiences. I knew the listeners were going to feel that shit in their souls. "Put those headphones back on; you 'bout to record the hook. Just wait for the beat to drop. Wait for it."

late twenties. They kept giving me stares, some of them rolling their eyes and shit. I didn't know them from a can of paint on a white Chevy. I was sure they knew me, everybody did. You didn't have to be high in rank to know where I came from and the gang I claimed. With me being sworn in as the Eastside Warriors' right hand, they didn't want to fuck with me like that. Because I could've snapped my fingers and Dre would've blown their brains back.

"Lex, come hang with the women. It ain't nothing but men over there." Keisha was the bitch who talked to Frank, Qbaby's first cousin and closest homie. She was a tall, slender, chocolate woman who liked shaking her ass on any and every song that played over the speakers. She was known for dancing at clubs for local artists who put on a show. Mainly dancing for the Voices of the Block crew, they were well known in town, put on the biggest shows and had the wildest parties. They tried recruiting Lyric a few times, but she turned them down though because Pop wasn't going to allow it. She was always putting her dreams on hold to please Pop, which made me happy to know she was back in the studio with Beatz trying to achieve her longtime dream of rising to the limelight as a rap star.

I gave Qbaby a kiss on the cheek and headed over to the porch where Keisha and her girls her. She and Nu were best friends and their other friend Natasha was just there. She wasn't fine like them, she was a big bitch, not the fine big bitches with a pretty face either. The kind of bitch who wore her hair any kind of way and dressed in too-small clothes. The bitch was loud ass fuck too, and let the entire hood hit her nasty ass. Having rules I had to follow, I still got word on everybody in the hood. People stayed filling my ears with the latest gossip on the streets.

"There she fuckin' is. Come on bitch, shake some ass." Keisha tried hyping me up. I was good at twerking and freestyle dancing, I just wasn't comfortable doing all that with them in my midst. I saw the kind of stares those hoes gave me on the regular. A part of me knew one of them was feeling Qbaby, age gaps weren't a thing for bitches like them. They fucked young and old niggas, long as they had somebody to fuck with and fuck on.

"Naw, I'm good. Y'all just act up while I watch." I sat on the porch railing. Never tried being goody two shoes; that wasn't who I was.

"You need something to get you going. Bitch we have all the shit that can take the edge off and get you going. You wouldn't even be sore no more. We all know Qbaby got a big dick, nigga have you crippled for days," Keisha said through a grin. I kept my eyes fixed on her. Qbaby hung around a lot of people, and I was aware he was experienced around the block. It's what most niggas in the hood did. That was their thing, they were free to do whatever they wanted. Long as the girls flocked to them, they weren't going to turn them down.

"I'm good, you just do your drugs and hop dick to dick." I had to get away from that bitch before I smashed her head in. But then something went through me. I had the right to beat a bitch down bad for trying to cross me or show me up. Pop never condoned us fighting with people who stayed in the hood; we were supposed to be one big family and be about unity. But I had to show the bitch not to fucking cross me long as I lived. Wasn't no way I was going to walk away and tuck my tail or bite my muthafuckin' tongue. The Eastside was under new management. "Bitch!"

I turned around and punched that bitch's front gold tooth down her throat. Then I followed up with a left hook to her temple. She fell right on her ass. Her girls tried to jump in, I was too fast with my Glock though. They backed away when they saw I was strapped.

"That's right, bitches. Don't ever cross me. You think I care 'bout who you fuck and all that shit? You better put some respect on my name hoe out here in these streets, my family runs the fuckin' show. So, bow down and fall in line." I walked off the porch in one piece. I was on a mission to slap Qbaby's grill down his throat. If he had bitches on the side, then they needed to fall in line. I wasn't having that shit. I came from a family that didn't do all the side chick drama. If Pop had other hoes on the side, it never came to the limelight even after he was dead. He made sure whatever he did away from home was handled.

"Nigga, you out your goofy ass mind having me around bitches you fuckin' with?" I punched Qbaby right in the face. He hopped up out his chair like he was ready to do something. When he recognized who had hit him, he calmed down, placing his hands in the air. He let me know he didn't want any problems.

"Lex, what fuck. What's wrong?" Qbaby grabbed me by the arm lightly. I wasn't the kind of girl to break down in front of a dude. I was pissed more than anything in the world.

"You have some fuckin' nerves to have me in the company of bitches you fuck with. You think I'm some young, dumb fool out here? You think just because my pop is dead, you can move in on me and take me fast? Nigga you got me mistaken for the wrong bitch." I pulled away from Qbaby before things went left for a second time.

"Aye, Lex, we have to go. It's urgent business at HQ," Dre came out of nowhere with his words. When he said something was popping off at HQ, I knew then I had to drop the argument with Qbaby for another day. Probably not an argument at all, I was too young to be dealing with relationships anyway. I had a team to help run.

"This ain't over nigga." I took quick strides away from him. Dre was ahead of me, he opened the door to the truck and let me slid in then he circled around the truck and hopped in. HQ was about to be seeing us very soon.

* * *

"I GOT HERE AS SOON I could, is everything okay?" I walked in the building like I was sliding on ice. Dre wasn't able to catch up with me. I was too damn fast when I was determined to get somewhere. Just like he had the pedal to metal, I had my feet to the concrete, trying my best not to fall flat on my face from the adrenaline that was crippling.

"T-Max and the others brought him. Tonight we avenge our pop and move on. Then we will sign our names in blood to be in alliance with the Black Gods, Young Dro's crew from ATL. We will rise and do the things Pop didn't want to do. This is our team, our family for the taking. It's about change, Lex. We're 'bout to change up this gang." Lyric embraced me then quickly released me from the tight embrace. Beatz was standing near the stairway with his hand in his pocket. I didn't read into the way he was acting much, but it looked like he was on edge or wanted to run the hell out of the building from overthinking.

"He's here. The bitch ass nigga is here?" I questioned, already moving past Lyric on a search to find that punk nigga who played both sides of the game. The nigga who swore his name in blood to the Eastside Warriors only to betray all of us. He fooled Lyric like he would watch over her when in reality he was the person she needed protecting from. Just like I blew his cousin away, that's exactly how I was going to do him if Lyric didn't beat me to it.

"Hold on, just wait." Lyric snatched me back to her. "He has to suffer first. Make him feel the pain first. Torture the nigga until tears come out his eyes."

"I don't have time for all of that. He needs to be blasted, Lyric. Fuck all that other shit. Just give him that one-way ticket out of this." Lyric and I never really disagreed on a lot of things. But that night we bumped heads after a little while. She wanted to do all that torture shit while I wanted to look him in the eyes and blast him away. "That's what he did to Pop, he dropped him without thinking twice. I don't want to think twice about it, Lyric. Just get it over with."

"She's right, Lyric. Let's just drop him and get it over with. Let's get on with our lives and stop allowing this to hinder us in any kind of way," Beatz chimed on the conversation. Beatz still wasn't on my best side since he played a part in Michael being dropped, although he didn't give those exact orders.

"I make these decisions. I understand that you two advise me along with T-Max, but this is personal for me. It's personal. He betrayed me in more ways than anyone has, ever. This is personal." Lyric pointed her finger at me then to Beatz. "Don't nobody understand all the shit I've been through while dealing with this."

"Fine, but after all the torturing you take him through, I call dibs on blasting him away without blinking an eye. Deal?" I reached out to shake Lyric's hand.

"Deal," Lyric agreed with the plan. We ended the discussion on good terms. She was going to make sure Osiris suffered at her hand, do all the things he inflicted on other people. Make him feel what he did to others. Then just like he pulled the trigger on Pop, I was going to do the same to him. Shoot him in the same place he shot Pop, make him slowly die and think about all the wrong he did.

BEATZ

Lyric ordered everybody in the room to give her space while she dealt with the beef that lied between her and Osiris. She told me and Lex straight up that the problem she had with Osiris was personal. She wanted him to suffer at her hand, for him to feel all the pain she'd been through when he hurt her. A part of me was upset that she was even giving him any of her energy. He didn't deserve that part of her. She should've washed her hands clean of him like Lex said and be done with it. Lyric was too damn good to stoop to his level. She was better than him in so many ways. She was better than me too.

"I bet you thought this day wouldn't come. That you would magically stay behind bars and fight to stay alive. Probably make friends and you take over the prison like you wanted to take over the streets. But you see none of that is going to happen now." Lyric circled the chair like she'd lost her mind. I'd never seen that part of her before. She was always the sweet, innocent girl that let karma force her enemies to bow to her feet. That was the person that I fell in love with. But seeing her in there taking control of the situation, made me love her more. Because I saw that she was able to take a stand in what she believed in. To face her enemies head-on and let them know that they were an enemy. I couldn't say I admired her for allowing Osiris to torture me the way he did. However, I understood where she was coming from in a way. Because I would want my enemies to pay for crossing me too. It's how shit went on the street; you crossed over a person high in power then you better prepare for that same person to cross you ten times over. To inflict all kind of pain on you while some of them go after your family and make you watch someone you love suffer. I heard crazy stories about what people in high power did to their foes. To be honest, I believed Lyric was letting Osiris off easy.

"How do you feel nigga?" Lyric smacked Osiris upside the head like he was a bitch sitting there. She was in charge and anybody watching could tell she called all the shots. We were just there to advise her like she said. That was all. And while I knew I could get my cheap shots in, she gave Lex the honors to end the nigga in cold blood.

"What are you waiting for, Lyric? You thinking 'bout sparing my life like you did that square nigga over there? You like giving people second chances thinking they can redeem themselves after going off the deep end. You think giving second chances will make you look like a damn god. But a real ass nigga like me don't give a fuck about all of that. You can put a bullet in my dome and I'm gone. I won't remember any of this shit, and the same goes for me if you allow me to walk," Osiris shot his words at Lyric as if she was a weak woman standing in his presence. In my eyes, she was much stronger than any person I'd ever come across. He thought bringing me up would take the heat off him. He was the center of attention though. What I did before him didn't matter at that time. He was the new public enemy number one, while I was given the chance to make things right between Lyric and I. We were on the road to achieving our dreams and building our new lives on loyalty and trust. Gaining her trust back was my main priority, and that's what I was doing. Little by little I was slowly showing she could trust me, that she had my trust and I would never betray her in that kind of way again.

"You think talking all that big talk will force me to give you the easy way out? It don't work that way Osiris. You will suffer for what you've done. You will pay for treason however long I see fit for your punishment." Lyric pulled out a pocketknife and brushed the knife against Osiris' neck from the back all the way to the front of his neck. Then out of nowhere, she shoved the knife into his right hand. The nigga didn't even flinch. He was determined to look like he was a real thug in there. He didn't want any of us to see him in pain. But I saw the scared ass look in his eyes. He was afraid of what kind of punishment Lyric was going to put him through.

"That's all you got? What kind of pussy shit is that? I know a little bitch in the hood that stabbed a nigga harder than that." Osiris broke down in a big chuckle. "Bring it on. I'm prepared to go out like I came in the world. I came out my mom duke's womb fighting for my life. And that's how I fuckin' plan to go out."

"I see." Lyric grabbed the hammer that rested on the floor. She got a tight grip around it; she drew it back then brought it to his left kneecap then to the right. She beat his legs up until there were no more bones to hear break. That time I was sure I saw a tear fall from Osiris' eyes as he bit down hard on his teeth. He brought the beast out of Lyric. She was making sure she didn't let up on him in there. Which made me pleased that she didn't do all that to me. I was thankful.

"That's all you got? Is that all you fuckin' got?" Osiris yelled out through anger. He was still stuck on going out like a thug when in reality, he had lost the upper hand. The streets viewed him as a traitor; he was willing to go through with a deal granted by the cops to bring down another team. He made several mistakes that landed him in his death chair.

"No, that's not it." Lyric grabbed the fishhook tied to some line. She went through his open flesh and sowed it up with the line, then she ripped it apart again. After she did that, Osiris fell into a plea. He then started begging for his life, apologizing for all the wrong he did to her.

"Lyric, I'm sorry. It was wrong of me for doing that to Don. For lying to you. You told me you loved me and damn, I felt the same. I still do. I'm sorry for crossing you and your family. I swear it to God," Osiris yelled at Lyric through a lousy way of expressing his guilt. I had to excuse myself during the whole thing for a second. It bruised a part of my heart to know that she actually told him that she loved him. We hadn't even been apart that long for her to fall that hard for the nigga. I knew I hadn't been the best friend or companion to her during that time. She was falling for another nigga while I was falling apart.

* * *

"You straight? I didn't get a chance to speak with you last night after you dipped while I was losing my mind in there. I guess I have more of Pop's ways than I thought." Lyric was sitting on the bed putting pen to paper writing the last verse to the song we both knew was a hit if she just continued to put in the work.

"I'm good. I just needed some air last night. Things got pretty bad in there. I never been the one to…" I trailed off. There wasn't any use in mentioning who I was before. Because watching her torture Osiris wasn't worse than me betraying my friend and playing a part in Michael's murder. The kid had a whole life ahead of him and because of my plans going left, he was murdered on the block that Don fought so hard to keep clean of gunplay.

"He deserved it and you know that. He stood by Pop's side only to end him. He saw the right opportunity that day and decided to strike. What I'm doing to him is his punishment for treason. That's how the streets work. You betray your own, you pay with your life." Lyric sounded insane. She just wasn't the girl I grew up with. The girl that I knew didn't condone street malice or believe in making someone suffer at her hand. My sweet, innocent Lyric had changed, and I should never stop blaming myself for that very reason. She had to change in order to carry out the duties of her dad, to somehow make him proud although he wasn't even there in the flesh.

"I know, and I'm not knocking you for any of that. He deserved the punishment put forth. I get it. It's just… You allowing all of this, this new life, your new role to change you. I don't want you to have to change to please all these people, Lyric," I let the words burst from the deepest part of my body. I wish saying all of that to her made me feel a hundred pounds lighter; it didn't though because I still felt like I was carrying the world on my shoulders. I was still carrying the blame before she found out Osiris was the one who really was against her and her family, her team. Mostly against her pop, plotting his downfall for a decade.

"Beatz, change is good. If I was the same Lyric from before, I wouldn't be able to make these kinds of decisions. To make my enemies suffer for treason. I wouldn't be able to sit in the room with men who have been running the streets since forever. I had to fuckin' change, it was the only way to cope with all of this. Don't judge me for changing for the better when everybody I loved did me in." Lyric hopped out the bed, leaving me alone in the room, regretting I opened my damn mouth about her turning into a different person. Her last words hit me deep. She forgave me, I just knew she would never forget the things that I did that troubled her soul. I was wrong for all that, and I told her that every chance I received.

"Damnit!" I tossed the cover to the floor. My whole life I'd been running from confrontation. Hiding behind everything. I couldn't do that anymore if I really wanted to be there for Lyric. I had to be transparent with her. To learn to stop always tucking my tail. With all the things I did in the last month, I knew I had heart to help her get through whatever she was facing. To man up and make it right. To make it right even if it would take a lifetime to help her get through it.

"Your mom needs to see you," T-Max said while standing in the living room with his hands resting behind his back like he was in the military. Lyric made sure to tighten down on security just in case somebody tried to make a hit on us like the last time. She allowed T-Max to stay in the house with us until further notice while Dre held a big part of following everybody around whenever we decided to go out to the store or anyplace away from home. She offered to put my momma under protection too, but I knew my momma would never agree to such a thing.

"Is everything alright?" I asked, trying to see if I should go after Lyric or get my ass dressed and head down to Mansfield to check on my momma.

"It's 'bout your dad." T-Max left those words to hang in the air. Chills went over my body, causing my muscles to tighten. She hadn't given me news on my dad since he'd been away so I knew it had to be bad.

LYRIC

Beatz was feeling pity towards Osiris, he was damn near begging me to put the damn bastard out of his misery. I couldn't do it that soon though, because like I told him and Lex before, it was personal between Osiris and me. He laid up with me, got me close to him. He swindled his way into my circle, into Pop's life over the years, only to be a damn snake in the end. All Pop did for him, helped out of those fuckin' charges, although he did it because he felt sorry for the misguided youth. My pop always had a weakness for strays and that very weakness cost him his life in the end. He should've let Osiris do his time in the big boy prison and be done with it.

"You're still not set on handing it over to Wayne, I see." Momma sat at the kitchen table going to down a bowl of cereal, some heart-healthy bullshit. I was in no damn mood to listen to her. She did the one thing that most honchos would've taken her life for. She went and spoke to my enemy.

"I won't hand it over to anyone. Pop fought for this. For the Eastside, for his team, his family, and giving it away will place a stake in his fuckin' legacy. Put an end to all the things he worked so hard for. Is that what you want, Ma? To bury all the things Pop worked his ass off for?" It was a fact that if she didn't stop bugging me on a decision that was already set in stone, I was going to be forced to get my own place. I was technically grown and making decisions on my own. The real reason I was trying to stand on mutual grounds with Momma was due to the fact Lex and Boni were still under her roof. She had them by law because they were children, and the only way I knew they were fully protected was if I was there almost every step of the damn way. I was looking out for them per Pop's dying wish and my natural instincts to protect them at all cost.

"Lyric, are you seriously hearing yourself? You want to continue to give up your freedom, your dreams, to keep your dad's hopes and dreams alive. I don't know a lot about living but that's not part of it. I wanted out of this life for the longest of time and now I have the opportunity if you just let it all go. Let's start anew. That's all I want for my girls. We don't have to continue to live like this." Momma just wouldn't let the shit go. My decision was final. I couldn't express enough how the Eastside Warriors kept us alive. Pop had a lot of enemies and soon as we removed our hand from the streets and moved away from the people who would go through hell and hot water for us, enemies were sure to come rushing in at once.

"I'm not trying to hold you here. If you want to go and start anew then that's on you. You want to risk something happening to Lex and Boni because of bad decisions then that's on you. Sometimes starting new isn't always the best decision when you don't know what comes along with it." I took a seat at the table with Momma. This was something we just had to get out in the air. Either she was in or she was fucking out. There wasn't any kind of between the lines. I knew if it came down to her choosing a new life, Lex wasn't going to go for it. We were both down for the ride, it was just the thought of Boni being unsafe that made me want to lay hands on Momma. During the most trying time she chose to be weak instead of poke her chest out and be a hand to the Eastside Warriors or hell, just fucking believe that I had the same pull like Pop out there on the streets, if not more since the 211s were under my wings repping for my team.

"Lyric why won't you fuckin' listen to me? Wayne is a good man." Momma tossed the bowl of milk and cereal across the kitchen. Her voice was loud as fuck in there. I was sure the neighbors heard all the noise. She was being aggressive with her approach that was going in one ear and out the fucking other.

"Wayne will not have this team and that's final. And this will be the last time you approach me about this. Don't make me feel threatened either because my mother or not, I will have you put down if you put me and my family in danger. Lex and Boni's lives depend on us keeping power in our hands, our entire Eastside family depends on it." I shook my head, unable to believe I was having that conversation with her again. Or the fact that she tried to sell me short, and kept telling me Wayne was a good man when so many people knew how dirty he was. "Don't you know how many teams are waiting for our downfall to go in our hood to take over? Enforce all their rules on the innocent until everybody is too damn afraid to speak up?"

"That's not your fight, Lyric. It's not. And to think I had some kind of hope for you and your life, that you'd be more than the hood, you would chase your dreams and make it out like you always talked about." Momma tried to get through to me by bringing up my career and all the plans I had. However, what she didn't know was that I had it all figured out and Beatz and I were already working on a song that was marketable.

"Drop it, okay? Just stop trying to force something that's not going to happen. This is my life. Pop believed that I could step up in his shoes and that's what I've done. I've brought two teams back together to stand in each other's presence as a family. And far as my career and dreams, I'm still working towards that too." Just like the last time, I dropped the conversation and was already over the bullshit. It wasn't getting either of us anywhere.

* * *

LEX WAS my appointed right hand since I knew her and knew she was for the team. We were both after keeping things the same in our hood and on our team that Pop worked hard for. However, I still needed someone who knew all there was to know about the streets to attend the meeting I had with Young Dro. And although T-Max and I started on a rocky path, we were slowly coming around to being good friends working towards the same goals for our team.

By word of mouth, I was aware that he was the biggest honcho in Georgia, and he ran the streets like the Messiah. Niggas bowed to his damn feet, they caught chills in his presence because he was just that cold. As much as he gave to the hood, he snatched shit right back up when niggas failed to act right. Young Dro was disliked by a lot of gangs because he was stepping on niggas' necks and shitting on their annual salaries.

"Aside from him being a bit arrogant, I haven't heard anything bad about him. Just make sure you let him do all the talking. I learned over the years to be observant. That's how you learn if a man is genuine or not." T-Max tucked his phone away when Dre pulled into the parking lot of the Horseshoe, the one place I thought I would never see again. It brought back terrible memories. Made me want to order Dre to turn the truck around and take me back to HQ to end Osiris' entire existence.

"There's nothing about arrogance that offends me." I clutched my satchel. Since I knew the meeting with Young Dro was going to be fancy, I made sure my team and I dressed for the occasion.

"Oh, I know that all too well because you can be arrogant as fuck yourself. Make a bitch want to snatch that blonde ass wig off her fuckin head." Lex shot me a shitty little smile and all I could do was laugh her off. She of all people knew how I got down when I was feeling myself. I made bitches hate me from a distance without even trying. It was like they were always finding a reason to dislike me and I swear they had the stupidest reasons in the damn world.

"Okay, don't do me." I slid out the truck on beat of Dre opening the door for me. I lived the fancy life when Pop was alive, well I tasted part of it whenever we were out of town. But to be in the big seat and niggas running to open doors for me and rushing to the store to pick up my dinner had me at an all-time high with the honcho life. I swear, it was power in my fingertips because all I had to do was snap my fingers and niggas went running.

"You're not staying out here. I need somebody behind us ready to blast a nigga just in case some shit magically hit the damn fan," I spoke to Dre firmly.

"Yes, ma'am." Dre locked the doors to the truck and headed in the hotel right behind us. T-Max was strapped along with Lex, but I needed all hands on deck to not to be caught slipping. I learned that shit quick after Pop was gunned down basically in front of me. In the split second I was carried into the hotel, Osiris shot him in cold blood and blamed it on Beatz. But what really got me was that Pop didn't even tell me to watch my back for Osiris, and I figured it was because he didn't even know his right hand was the one to pull the damn trigger.

"Remember, let him do all the talking while we all listen to the fine details," T-Mac instructed for the second time. I heard him loud and clear the first time but I respected him for making sure I was paying attention and we all were following the plan we hashed out from the jump.

"I'm on it like green on a pickle." I shook my head at my horrible modifier. I was usually good at shit like that, not that day though. My brain was literally mashed potatoes due to overthinking. Young Dro was big in the game and all I wanted was to make a good first impression and seal a deal that would benefit all of us in the long run.

"Right this way." With my thoughts running around in my mind, I wasn't even aware that we were already inside of the restaurant and were being led to the table of our acquainted party. The Horseshoe had a nice five-star restaurant that wasn't my exact taste in food but it was good for meetings.

I followed behind the short Mexican lady who had on a tight black dress and knee-high, white boots. She had to be pushing her late fifties and was dressed like she was fresh off her shift at a strip club. I had to stop myself from laughing out loud and keep the thoughts to my damn self. Because my words would've come out all damn wrong inside of that place.

Once we were at the table, I took a seat in front of a tall, slender, light-skinned man and Lex was right beside me. I made sure she stayed close to me at all times. Dre sat four tables behind us and if Young Dro was coming like people said he would, I was sure he had some of his men sitting in the back too for his protection.

"You're more beautiful in person." The head honcho himself grabbed my hand and planted a kiss on it. He was breathtaking to almost any woman in passing. I had to admire him from a distance though. I wanted to get me and Beatz back where we used to be without any distractions.

"Thank you, you don't look half bad yourself." I pulled my hand away from him and put my game face on. T-Max told me to stay focused and to listen to every detail; it was part of the small plan we hashed out the night before.

"That nigga in front of you is one of my right hands and he goes by the name Haven. I know it sounds gay as hell but trust me, he earned that by saving niggas from some of the most violent situations. Word is, he has a heart of gold." Young Dro finally took a seat by his right hand, well one of his right hands. He operated with a heavy team of men who were in high power too.

"Nice to meet you both. That's T-Max over there, my adviser and she's Lex, my new appointed right hand and also my little sister," I said.

Young Dro and Haven stayed quiet for a moment right before breaking out in laughter. I knew it was the whole Lex being my right hand that made them laugh. But it wasn't a joke and my team was serious and still running shit. The least they could've done was show her an ounce of respect. She was young hands down, we both were young, but that still didn't take away how we were going to run the state. We both had a head on us, and that's what was going to get us to the top of the street life.

"What's so funny?" Lex opened her mouth. She never was the last to speak up for herself. She stayed ten toes down behind her name and I was always going to be there for her no matter what. "Last I checked I brought a nigga to his death bed behind Lyric and the team. And will do it again in a heartbeat. Just because I'm not the usual right hand or the kind you will have on your team does not make me anything less."

"My bad, it's just…I've never seen this before. It's like two children running a gang," Young Dro expressed his true feelings towards the new management of the Eastside Warriors and I wasn't expecting anything less coming from a person like him. He could've felt however he wanted, but I wasn't going to sit through any disrespect.

"I see where this is going and I'm excusing myself and my team. When you're serious about doing business and not with the petty shit, get at me. Until then, get your shit together." I stood from the table first with Lex following my lead and T-Max right behind us prepared to dip.

"Okay, fine. My apologies. I really want to do business with your team. I do. And I can assure you this isn't how I conduct business. It was unprofessional of me to laugh in your presence." Young Dro looked at me with sympathy in his eyes. I felt it was genuine, so I gestured Lex and T-Max to reoccupy their seats while I did the same.

"Fine, but make this meeting quick. You've stepped on my fuckin' bad side," I said.

"It will only take second." Young Dro grabbed a green folder from Haven and he went straight in with the pitch. The pitch that was either going to hook me in as a potential partner or push me away without any future of us ever working together in any kind of way.

"The Warriors are a big team, well, a huge team now since the 211s are incorporated. Your team trades in places that mine doesn't and vice versa. If we rule together, two honchos with one team, we'll be the biggest gang in the states. More money and ton more power." Young Dro viewed me for a moment then he slid a piece of paper across the table. I knew T-Max told me to do minimal talking during the meeting, but I had to let Young Dro know just how the fuck my team operated and I sure as hell wasn't going to allow him to be head of nothing to my team. If he wanted to swear allegiance, I was down.

"I will never give that kind of power to anyone to have over my team. More money sounds good, power too. But I will not have anyone ruling beside me as an equal on my team. Have you ever heard of two kings ruling?" I said, refusing to look over at T-Max, who I knew was shaking his head at my sudden reply instead of allowing Young Dro to talk himself into a hole.

"Two kings, I haven't, but a king and queen, I've seen many times." Young Dro flashed his gold teeth at me. Osiris had taught me a thing or two. To steer clear of thugged out niggas because they were ruthless and would do anything to stay on top. I was about street life, just not the street niggas who thought they would take my company, my team and make it their own because they figured they were more streetwise than me. That they could run my team better than I could. If I wanted to be the biggest team in the states, I could've made that possible without making a deal with Young Dro. Power wasn't something I wanted, because I already had it; now making more money was what I was looking for.

"But I ain't no queen. I'm the hood princess and I will rule my team how I see fit. You can be in alliance with my team. We can trade like sisters and brothers, we can even meet up to chop up business from time to time. That's it though." I reached out to shake Young Dro's hand, letting him know there wasn't anything left on the table to discuss. Our meeting was adjourned.

OSIRIS

I was on my last damn leg in that room. Lyric had done everything in the book to me plus more. At first I tried to show her that I wasn't a pussy and could take my punishment. Then I found myself begging for my damn life. I wasn't supposed to go out like that. The cops were supposed to protect me at all cost. I was their possession. At least that's how they put it before they allowed my ass to walk out a free man. I kept going over shit in my head. Like was there something I could've done to prevent my situation. I wasn't able to come up with anything though. Don was the reason my brother died at an early age for making an honest mistake and I was that bad karma that God put in his presence. All Don's bad was going to catch up with him someday, I just got him before the rest of his bad could pay him a visit. I was a bold ass nigga out there. I did the one thing that most niggas only talked about amongst themselves.

"Today you get granted your one-way ticket out. Do you have any last words?" Lex closed in the small distance between us. Over the years of observing Lex, I had no doubt that she was going to grow up to be ruthless just like Don. See, Lyric was pushed to her limits and it made her not care about people who wronged her. While Lex didn't give one fuck about anyone, she believed in making people pay for their sins. I remember Don telling me about all the fights she kept getting into at school. And how she was always the one to throw the first punch on someone else's behalf.

"Last words…you really want to hear my last words?" I thought long and hard on what I wanted to say before she busted a cap through my head or wherever she planned to place one.

"I really don't, I just thought I should give the option since this will be your last time ever speaking on his earth." Lex viewed me with a smug expression. I knew they had fucked me up. I think they did me more damage than I had ever done to another person during my entire reign as Don's right hand. Because in most cases, he wanted us to get it over with and be done with it. They weren't Don though, and the bad blood between us was personal. Especially Lyric and me. I got in her head then in her underwear. I was wrapping her around my finger with every chance I received. She even fell in love with a nigga.

"I would like to speak my last words to Lyric," I spoke during the worse pain I'd ever experienced in my entire life. If I had a say in my punishment, I would've put an end to my pain days ago. The whole time during the punishment I kept seeing my mom duke's face. I felt comfort in the midst of my pain. It was like she was there holding my hand to get through all the torment. I was no damn saint and I knew I didn't deserve any one of them to take it easy on me. It was clear as day that I dug my own damn grave; they were just one second away from burying my ass six feet under.

"You don't get that kind of privilege, nigga." Lex laughed in my face like she was Satan himself. I didn't know what would become of her, but she was going to make a lot of people's hearts ache over the years. Lex was going to be a force to be reckoned with. And she was going to wear the title of ending my life once and for all. They were going to praise her for her bravery, have a party in the accomplishment of my death.

"You know, since no one else is in here, I guess I can be honest with you." Lex circled around me like the crazy girl that she was. She'd lost her mind the day her friend was murdered in front of her. "I thought 'bout murdering Pop too. I even shot at him in his own home for beating on my momma like a punching bag. And that day he made me his public enemy number one. His own daughter was his enemy. I wasn't able to make things right between the two of us, or put the damn past behind us because you took him before I was able to do all of that."

Lex pulled the Glock 19 from her waistband; it didn't take her any time to cock the lever back and pull the trigger. She blasted me in my right shoulder without blinking an eye. I never knew she and Don had any bad blood. It never was my business to know any of that. I didn't even know he laid hands on Brier either. Don kept his personal life personal. And me being me, I never tried to learn anything concerning his personal life. It was his business.

"I was eventually going to come back around. We were going to put it all behind us; you took that away from me though. The demon in you made sure you robbed me of any opportunity of reconciling. Do you know how much that hurts?" Lex shot me again in the same damn wound. I don't how the hell she had an aim that sharp to hit in the same spot twice, but she did. She was making sure I paid the highest price on her behalf. Lyric was hurt because of the false love and hope I gave her while Lex was furious that Don was dead, and she couldn't beg his forgiveness for stepping up to him.

"The beef between Don and I didn't have anything to do with you or Lyric. He had my brother murdered and thought he was going to get away with it by taking a naïve teenager under his wings to try and right his wrong. It don't work that way, Lex. It just don't. If somebody had Lyric killed, how far would you go to avenge her?"

"I would turn every stone in America, bring pain to the families of the people involved, make them suffer, then I would pull the trigger and blast them." Lex held the gun in her hand firmly, finger around the trigger.

BANG! BANG! BANG! BANG!

LEX

I stared at Osiris' limp body, while my veins slowly iced over. I pulled the trigger on somebody before, that was when I was afraid for Lyric's life and my own damn safety, so I did what had to be done. I felt different after I shot Osiris though. I was feeling guilt that I had no right to feel. He was the enemy and if that didn't give me the damn right to take his life, I didn't know what did. He pulled the trigger on Pop and turned a blind eye. He still fucked with our circle, standing beside Lyric during the funeral and even after. He played his role very fucking well. What I gave him was what he deserved. It had to be.

I walked out of the room with the blood on my conscience. It was Lyric's idea for us to torture him. I just called dibs on ending him. Although Beatz was up for it in the beginning, he slowly got himself out of it altogether. And judging from the way I was feeling, I understood why he steered clear of it. Killing Osiris wasn't satisfying how I imagined, it didn't fill that numbness inside of me. I still felt empty and lost.

"It's done?" Lyric shot me a satisfied smirk. Removing Osiris from her life, away from the earth, was what she needed. Lyric had gone through a lot during a short amount of time. She'd trusted people who weren't worthy of her trust and she looked out for them when they weren't even trying to look out for her. My sister had a heart of gold and there was no denying it. However, she managed to learn quickly how to have a heart of gold while not being walked over and stomped on.

"Yeah, it's done. He's dead. Now we can move on, Lyric. All of this hurt can be behind us for once. We rule the Eastside our way," I said. Pop did his part out there on the streets. I couldn't say he did all that was right within his power. It was time for us to step up though, to make the streets know our names and not just by hearing our pop's name.

"Good, it's time for a fuckin' celebration." Lyric grabbed my hand and led me out of the building. She was celebrating Osiris being banished from the streets, from the fuckin' earth at my hand. I knew since Osiris was gone and we were doing business with other crews, sending out peace offerings, everything was going to soon be smooth sailing and my deeds toward Osiris would really mean something. It would all be worth it because we would have the world in the palm of our hands with one less enemy to deal with. One less public enemy that is.

"Don't we have to get the body moved first?" Osiris sitting in the warehouse dead, surrounded by blood, was nowhere near a good idea.

"I'll have one of the men to get rid of him. Don't worry about all of that. He's dead, no cops are going to come looking for him and if they do, then we just have somebody to place a bullet in their heads, or threaten their families. Whatever gets them back in line." Lyric was a completely different person from a month ago, hell, even just a day ago.

"Alrighty then," I said, not even expressing what I was feeling. We'd made a vow to keep the Eastside alive and to walk in Pop's footsteps. I was only sixteen and sworn as Lyric's right hand, to loyally serve as the right hand to the Eastside Warriors. It was a big world out there no doubt, but we had to stay alive long enough to see it. Lyric couldn't stress to me enough the importance of keeping the upper hand, to make sure we kept a foot in the game because the moment we let up off our enemies' necks, the streets were going to come for us without a second thought. It's how things worked out there.

I slid in the truck, not even dressed for any kind of celebration. I had just offed Osiris, probably had specks of blood on my flesh. I was in no condition to be seen by the public with adrenaline still running through my veins.

"Have you heard from Beatz since the other morning?" I tried my best to put my mind on anything except what I had done. It didn't take long for me to feel better either.

"Yeah, a text here and there. He's dealing with something concerning his pop. It has to be deep since he hasn't been back over to the house or even to HQ. I'm actually kind of worried but I know I have to keep a move on if I want the team to operate to standards." Lyric strolled through her phone without looking over at me. Lyric wasn't ever the kind of person to stayed glued to any electronic device if it didn't have anything to do with her music. "I did something really crazy."

"Crazy like what?" I side-eyed Lyric. Torturing Osiris was crazy, letting Beatz go without knowing the full story was crazy. I didn't think the news she was about to lay on me was anything close to any of those things, but I still braced myself for what she had to say.

"I posted a video of me on Instagram rapping a verse from my new single and people are eating it up. Beatz didn't lie. People are calling me the next Queen of Rap." Lyric handed me her phone. I went straight to the comments, and low and behold, she was like an overnight sensation. For a while, I thought she would never wake up to chase her dreams or get anywhere close to fulfilling them. It took for us to lose Pop and go through a whole lot of other tribulations for her to even consider taking her dreams serious.

"Damn, if you keep this up, you can be the new face of female rap. The face of new, raw hood rap. You won't be the face of some diluted rap, you too sick for that shit." I handed the phone back to Lyric.

"Thank you. I have to give it to Beatz though, if it wasn't for him…if it wasn't for him giving me that extra push, none of this would be happening right now." Lyric tucked her phone away. Silence crept over us until T-Max hopped in the truck and played his old school rap music too damn loud. I fucked with the old school music heavily, but he was overdoing it. If he didn't turn it down, my ears probably were going to start bleeding.

"Aye, turn that shit down. I would love to hear my own thoughts," I yelled out loud enough for T-Max to hear over the music.

"Oh, my bad. I thought we were in a celebration mood." T-Max quickly turned down the radio, turning his attention to the task at hand, getting us from HQ to wherever the hell the party was being held at.

"You straight?" Lyric finally opened her mouth to ask me the one question I was dreading. I wasn't okay; I hadn't been okay for a long time. I'd been carrying the world on my shoulders for the longest time. Hiding my true feelings, keeping them buried six feet under.

"I'm just a bit shaken up is all. I never just pulled the trigger to pull it," I expressed.

"You'll get used to it," T-Max chimed in.

"Was I talking to you?" I snapped at T-Max soon as those words escaped his mouth.

"He deserved all of that, Lex. You've done nothing wrong," Lyric said. I kept replaying her words in my head. *He deserved it.*

* * *

I STEPPED AWAY from the big ass party that Lyric hosted; she even preformed and the crowd went crazy. She really was blowing up by the days that crept by. Before we all knew it, my sister was going to be a superstar that came straight from the hood, the only superstar that I knew personally that owned and operated one of the biggest street gangs in the state of Louisiana.

Qbaby had entered the spot and I was in no kind of headspace to even speak to the two-timing nigga. He had me all fucked up. I wasn't having any of that bullshit. If he was fucking with Keisha then he was fucking with the bitch. All he had to do was tell me what it was and I would've happily stepped my happy ass back. Besides, what I shared with him was to get my mind off Michael in the first place. To somehow cope with his death, to get rid of the empty feeling that nothing was able to fill. Then on top of all of that, Qbaby seemed different. He was a street nigga but a bit clean cut around the edges. He didn't have a family to lean on, nobody but himself. He was a damn hustler and I respected that about him. He swooped me up off my feet, persuading me to let my guard down like I did around no other. He was honestly a stranger in passing before the day we exchanged numbers. Standing outside of that building, I wished there was a way to redo the entire day.

"Lex, can I just talk to you for a minute? Just for a minute I swear." Qbaby was already getting too damn close to me. He needed to stay at least five feet away from me. If he came any closer I was afraid I would knock his front teeth down his throat along with that grill he flashed around every ten minutes.

"Have a word after you played me like a fuckin' fool? You was fuckin' with that bitch the entire time while I walked around like a damn dumb ass bitch out there. You know who the fuck I am, what my people all about. How the hood is down for me, even the muthafuckas who act all haterish. Yet you still played me with my eyes wide open." I let everything out without trying to hold back. He had to hear my damn wrath. To know how bad he'd fucked up and how I wasn't set on letting any of it go. He crossed a line no other nigga crossed. He played me for a young fool.

"Lex, Keisha is in the past. Part of my past. I hadn't messed with her in a whole year. She fucks with my good homie now. Whatever she told you was all lies. It's not my intentions to play you like that. I just want to love you, to receive the love I never had, that's all. I don't have any other motives. I swear it," Qbaby sounded all sincere. I wasn't trying to hear it though. Even if he wasn't fuckin' Keisha, he should've told me that they had history and to watch out for her. Plus, I was too damn young to be falling in love and shit. I had a whole lot of other things on my plate. I still was trying to figure out what path to take in life. Having a nigga all in my life wasn't going to allow me the space to do that.

"Look, I just can't get caught up in all of that. In whatever you have going on. I have a lot of shit on my plate already. I'm still grieving the loss of my best friend and my pop. All this relationship shit is for the birds. If it's meant to be somewhere down the road, then it's meant. But I'm done with it and that's the end of it," I said what I wanted, the conversation was over. I didn't have time to hear him out or to listen to any of the words that sounded good.

"Okay, I respect that. I wish you nothing but the best." Qbaby wiped his left hand across his mouth as he walked away. My heart never was invested in him, so letting go was easy to me.

Right after he walked away, Moomoo walked up. I hadn't spoken to her since the day she got all fly with me. She kept pushing herself towards me, trying to get on me when I wasn't swinging that way with her. She was my damn friend and I just wanted to keep it that way.

"Too soon for reconciling?" Moomoo held her arms out as she kept walking towards me. She embraced me without any further words. And I swear it felt like my soul had been needing that hug for a long time. It was nice standing on mutual grounds with my best friend even after our differences. She loved me in her own little way while I loved and cared for her like a sister. With Lyric and her standing beside me, I was going to be able to get my life together to somehow manage my mental state. They weren't Michael but I was sure he was watching over me from somewhere and proud that I managed to let someone else in besides him.

BEATZ

The news was laid on me a few days ago about my dad committing suicide in prison. There was no footage of what happened in there. Nothing. Tell us why the hell he decided to end his life or what he was going through. I hadn't spoken to him since he was incarcerated but my heart, the pain, all of it cut deeper than a butcher's knife.

Lyric kept texting me on and off since I'd been missing in action; she wanted to know if everything was alright. If I was being honest with myself, I felt like I was reaping some bad karma. Like maybe God wanted me to feel Lyric's pain because I was being insincere when Don was shot. Or maybe he wanted me to pay for my sins because I was part of the reason Don was dead. It was a slap in the face, a bullet to the heart.

"I wasted all these years, all these years because of you not allowing me to write to him. Or to go visit when the courts allowed it. What am I supposed to do now? He probably died thinking I hated him. I didn't hate him for anything he did. He had to show niggas not to cross him," I said with anger beating at my temples.

My momma did some messed up shit behind his back, and the moment he found out, he lost his cool. One simple mistake cost him everything. Instead of letting it go, moving on to start over, he lashed out. He murdered a man and was serving time. He was a tough man, I just never thought he would be so empty to end his own life.

"Blame me if you must, Rashad. Blame me because I'm guilty of stepping out after years of not feeling loved. Your dad couldn't handle what he dished out and that wasn't my problem. When I found out he was cheating on me with all those lil' hood hoes running around the streets, I kept my shit together. I prayed about it until I couldn't pray anymore. Then I fell into the arms of a man that showed me something different. If I'm so damn bad then that's my problem," Momma said. She wasn't sad about my dad being dead; to me she was counting it as a blessing or something.

"Did you really have to force me not to keep in touch with him? You know how many nights I wondered about the wisdom he could've laid on me during my roughest days? All I wanted was for my dad to be there." Even in my anger I knew I couldn't stay mad at Momma for long because it wasn't wholly her fault. I just needed someone to direct my anger towards. Momma and Dad hadn't lived in the same house in ten years or so, and they still were married. She hadn't brought a man home, and I never saw her with a man after what happened. I don't know if she was just good at hiding her relationships or just downright fed up with men after what happened all of those years back.

"Rashad, nobody is really to blame for any of this. Your dad chose his own path in life. I said blame me because I want you to be able to take your frustration out on somebody, but I am not to blame for what he did. Now you can either love me or hate me. That's your choice." Momma giving up the argument with me could be heard in her voice. She sounded about five seconds away from bursting into tears. It made my heart cry out for her. She'd been holding everything down since Dad got locked up for reckless behavior. Raising me from then until this very moment. When the Eastside Warriors came down on my head, she handed me her life savings along with her only car just so I could be safe. She had a heart of gold, but she somehow got caught up in a scandalous act. I just had to give her props during both of our grief. I knew she was taking it hard herself. I had to pull myself together to be there for her through such a terrible time.

"It's just...I wasted so much time. I never got the chance to speak with him after all of that went down. I just wanted to speak with him." I broke down in front of my momma. Death was hitting every other week it seemed like. I just prayed it stopped so everybody could get back to normal.

"I know, baby. I know. And I'm sorry for forcing you to steer clear of him. I just wanted you to go on and live a normal life without worrying about him being locked up. I was trying my best to protect you, not knowing I was hurting you altogether. I'm sorry." Momma draped her arms around me and we sobbed together.

* * *

AFTER AVOIDING Lyric and the whole world, I decided to finally show my face. Momma was dealing with all the arrangements for the funeral while I got my head straight. If it was left up to me, he probably would've been left in the morgue until the mortician grew tired and did something with the corpse. I wasn't brave enough to go face anything like that. Seeing him dead like that, making plans to put him in the ground, it wasn't my cup of tea. That kind of tea was far too strong.

"I was afraid you made a run for it." Lyric handed me a cup of whiskey. That celebration I had at Wayne's spot a few weeks back, made me frown at the thought of any kind of alcohol. I had to do it for her though, we were celebrating her finally fully rising to the throne as honcho. The HBIC, the only woman I knew who could run a gang and chase after her dreams the way she did. She went hard for her career in the past; she was throwing herself out there now though. She wasn't afraid of any form of criticism. I told her to post a teaser on the internet and she did exactly that; she received a lot of good feedback from listeners.

I was even receiving messages from other producers who wanted to work with her and me. Then on top of all that, she grabbed the opportunity to showcase herself in front of the crowded building of people at the victory celebration. Almost everybody from our hood was present. We were in a building filled with familiar faces along with a group of people who weren't familiar. Lyric did fill me in about all of that. I didn't have to be the smartest to know that the people who weren't from our block in attendance were Young Dro and his crew out of Atlanta. He was an important man. He and the Eastside Warriors were standing on mutual grounds. With them working alongside each other with ex-members of the 211s backing them, they hatched a plan to get rid of Wayne in a slick way that wouldn't point back to either team because Lyric found out that he was the one who had us shot at.

"Naw, I'm not running from anything. Observing you, I learned to just face everything head-on and make a plan as I go." I grabbed her into my arms, disposing of the cup of whiskey in the process. I was facing a terrible time in my life, so I had to be completely sober to face it if I ever wanted to truly get over it.

"What's really going on with you? I've been knowing you long enough to know when something is eating at you. What's going on?" Lyric lightly broke away from my embrace. She looked up at me with questions written all in her eyes.

"My dad committed suicide in prison. I hadn't spoken to him since he was arrested for the crime. My momma made sure we weren't in attendance at any of the hearings and that I stayed clear of writing him any letters or going to any authorized visit." Lyric knew the rundown on my family history; me not being able to communicate with my dad wasn't something new to her. I opened up to her about the issue over the years, and she gave me good advice on more than one occasion. Some advice I regretted not taking. Had I listened to her, I wouldn't have taken his death so hard. Because then we would've had some form of communication by me writing a simple letter within those long ten years.

"I'm sorry for your loss," Lyric said.

"No, don't. I don't deserve your sympathy when I wasn't there during your loss. I'm going to be alright, Lyric," I replied in search of that drink I ditched a few moments prior to our conversation.

"Beatz, you were pressured into joining the 211s. I hurt you just like you hurt me. We've both wronged each other. But that doesn't mean we can't right our wrong by doing right by each other moving forward. I don't hold any grudge against you. I want to be here for you, Beatz, just how you've been here for me when you found out Osiris was against me and the crew. You could've turned a blind eye after what I had done to you but you didn't. And to me, that speaks volumes." Lyric embraced me again planting a kiss in the process. It all felt right. I felt safe being there with her, although she was the woman and I was a man. Lyric was strong, just the kind of woman I needed in my corner rooting for me.

"Lyric, I love you," I let those words rip from my soul. The way things were looking in the hood, I could've turned the corner the following day and got dropped. The weeks ahead weren't promised to any of us. She had to know how I felt about her then and there without any holding back. Life could throw hellfire at us, but I wasn't set on running away again and making rash decisions.

"I love you too. I've loved you since forever and I wish to keep loving you for another lifetime," Lyric replied. We were young with our entire lives ahead of us, we'd trialed and errored, and I was sure there would be more but with her standing beside me, I could somehow survive three lifetimes more with her love alone.

NOTE FROM AUTHOR K.A. WILLIAMS

Thank you for your continued support. I hope I was able to fulfill your literary cravings as usual.

To stay in the loop with what I'm working on and all of my nail-biting short stories, please follow me on my social media accounts below.

ABOUT THE AUTHOR

K.A. Williams is an Urban Romance author signed with Royalty Publishing House. She also published Historical Fiction novels under her company Storytellers Publication, allowing her to express her passion for African American history while at the same time putting glamour on Urban life.

K.A. Williams made her debut in the literary industry back in 2012 at only sixteen years old with the release of *The Forbidden Truth* and *Jake's Lineage* short story trilogy. K.A. Williams has written over twenty books over the span of five years.

K.A. Williams is also a screenplay writer, adapting her novel *Jake's Lineage* into a movie with pending casting dates.

K.A. Williams resides in Mansfield, Louisiana with her husband and daughter.

Stay Connected:
Facebook Group: K.A. Williams' Readers Circle

facebook.com/AuthorK.A.Williams
twitter.com/kawilliams_
instagram.com/k.a._williams

OTHER BOOKS BY THE AUTHOR

Dirty Secrets & Broken Bottles

Falling Hard for a Savage 1-3

Lovin' A Thug Till My Last Breath

Intoxicated by Hood Love 1-4

Falling for His Savage Love 1-3

Lovin' The Godfather of the Streets 1-3

Lovin' A Jamaican Godfather

Hood Princess: An Eastside Love Story

Massa's Baby

Fragments of Autumn

Jake's Lineage

Afterlife

Dolly and Moe